TEMPLARS QUEST

GHOST KILLER

BOOK ONE OF THE TEMPLARS QUEST CHRONICLES

Another Jack Gunn Adventure Series

THOMAS H. WARD

TEMPLARS QUEST:

Ghost Killer

BOOK #1 THE TEMPLARS QUEST CHRONICLES

by

THOMAS H. WARD

ISBN-13: 978-0692506189
ISBN-10: 0692506187

This book is a work of fiction. Names, characters, and incidents are a product of the author's imagination or used fictitiously. Any resemblance to persons, living or dead is entirely coincidental.

Transcendent Publishing
www.transcendentpublishing.com

TABLE OF CONTENTS

INTRODUCTION

Over the past two years we have been in continuous battles to protect our way of life on Tocabaga. We are living in a utopia compared to other poor souls who weren't so lucky. Maybe they didn't plan for the collapse like we did, or maybe they wanted the government to take care of them.

We dare not venture too far from Tocabaga because it's a mean cruel world out there. The furthest we have ever traveled is about 120 miles north of here, on a hunting trip to Bushnell countryside. That's where we met the Knights Templar for the first time. We had no idea that the Knights Templar still existed. I'll never forget the date because things changed forever after that day. It was August 3, 2025.

This is a strange story, but true. My small group of hunters happened to come upon the

Knights Templar, at four in the morning, who were camped on the side of the road. An old man came up to me and asked if we could spare any food. I didn't know it at the time, but he was Jack de Molay, the Grand Master of the old Knights Templar.

We had never met before, but somehow he knew my name. Jack de Molay told me this bizarre story that God had sent me to protect his grandchildren, Adam and Emma. It was strange because my loyal guard dog, Adolf, was friendly to them and usually he does not take to strangers.

Old man Jack asked me to take care of the kids until they were older. He wanted them to have, as he called it, a more or less normal life. Jack went to rest in his car, telling me he would advise more details later, after a short nap.

Unfortunately he passed away in his sleep with my dog sitting next to him, who let out a howl noting his departure from this earth. We buried him on the roadside and the children ended up coming with me to Tocabaga, because according to Jack, it was God's will.

I had no choice but to follow his wish, and adopted twelve-year-old Adam and nine-year-old Emma. I'm a pushover when it comes to taking care of kids. I have already adopted six children. I took them off the streets of death and brought them to live with my family where they could grow up without fear. They would grow up like normal children with a caring family, and a community to help guide them.

They'd never be hungry again. Without children there is no future for Tocabaga, or for the United States to survive.

Young Adam de Molay has now become the Grand Master of the modern Templar Warriors. A new adventure is beginning. We are preparing to proceed on the Templars Quest.

I can't explain it, but I was compelled, or for lack of a better word, commanded to take up this journey, by a higher power.

My name is Jack Gunn and these are my chronicles.

The year is 2026 and we have survived over two years living on Tocabaga Island since the collapse of the government. I live here with my entire family. The real name of this island will not be disclosed, nor the location. Tocabaga is a clue as to our general location. It is a sanctuary where one can be safe from what is going on in the outside world. If you happen to come here, are of good character, and believe in Constitution, you are welcome to stay. The current population is 556 people. We help each other stay alive.

I was elected Vice President and Director of Security on Tocabaga because no one else wanted the job, or maybe because I have the most experience in security matters. I won't hesitate to terminate anyone who is a threat to our community.

I am the oldest of three Brothers. We grew up fighting bullies and gang members in a tough neighborhood in south Chicago. My Dad, one of the most honest men I have known, always stressed tell the truth, and help each other. Never ever be a bully, never steal, and try to protect those who cannot protect themselves. I have always stood up for the people who could not defend themselves. I hate liars and bullies.

Standing 6 feet tall at 180 pounds, I'm in great shape for my age and my body is honed by years of physical training. I keep in shape by lifting weights almost every day and running three miles, four times a week. I shave my head two times a week as it is cooler with no hair in the hot south. I sport a gray mustache and goatee that I keep well-trimmed and short. There is a two-inch scar on my forehead from a knife fight years ago.

I spent four years in the Army as a Military Policeman, and became an expert in the use of handguns, rifles, shotguns, and in hand-to-hand combat. My legs have skin grafts from burns due to an explosion when I worked for the DOD (Department of Defense) doing security work for seven years. I always carry my Glock 17, and Black Bear Cold Steel fighting knife, no matter where I go.

I love our country, freedom, my family, and friends. If anyone messes with my family, or friends, justice will be swift and painful. I have no use for anyone who breaks the law, cheats or steals. For the most part I follow the Ten Commandments, but also believe in The Code of Hammurabi, which is an eye for an eye. I fight to keep our Bill of Rights under the United States Constitution.

Now, I am fighting alongside the Templar Warriors to find the lost treasure. We are following the clues of a holy relic named the 'Sword of Jerusalem.' The Arc of the Covenant, designed by God, and made by man, is one of the holy items we are seeking. Whoever finds the treasure could very well control the destiny of the United States.

REMENISCING

I'll never forget what happened on September 14, 2025. That's the day that Adam de Molay became the Grand Master of the new Templar Warriors. It's the day that either Adam, God, or an Angle killed Adam's uncle, Christian de Molay, using the Sword of Jerusalem. It was the weirdest and most supernatural event I have ever witnessed.

Adam de Molay is a descendent of a long line of Templar Knights. His bloodline dates back to Jacques de Molay, who was the last Grand Master of the Knights Templar. Rumor has it that Jacques hid the treasure taken from Jerusalem. In 1314 the King of France had him burned at the stake for not revealing where the treasure was hidden. The King coveted the long lost Templars Treasure and searched for it in vain, all over Europe.

As I was making final preparations for our

long trip to search for the holy treasure, I thought back to that day. This is an account of what happened.

On September 13, 2025, a man named Christian de Molay showed up, out of nowhere, at our gate which secures the entrance to the Tocabaga Bridge. There was an entourage of twenty four men with him and they were well armed. He wanted custody of Adam and Emma claiming to be their uncle. If he was their uncle then he was entitled to lawful custody. However, he also wanted the Sword of Jerusalem.

After discussions with Adam, I believed Christian was a dangerous person who would do harm to Adam and use the holy sword to his advantage. I made a plan with my men, to terminate Christian the next day, if he wouldn't listen to reason.

Since Adam and Emma didn't really know their uncle, and had only seen a picture of him, he was a stranger. Both children wanted to stay with my family as their real grandfather had wanted them to do.

The next morning, September 14, 2025, I sat in the kitchen thinking about my plan to negotiate with Christian, or to terminate him, when Adam walked in and gave me a hug. "Grandpa, I don't want you to get killed protecting me."

"Adam, don't worry, I'm not gonna get killed. You're part of my family. On Tocabaga we're all family. The one thing I do know is how to protect my family. Besides, I think God is on our side."

"More than you may think, Grandpa."

My radio hissed. "Jack, you better come down to the

gate. Christian de Molay is demanding to talk to you and Adam."

I checked my watch; it was only 10:30 am. "Ok, I'll be right there."

Adam said, "Don't go."

I replied, "You stay here with Adolf, and I'll go talk to him." I left the dog with Adam so it wouldn't be a distraction during a possible gun battle.

Twenty minutes later, taking my time, I approached the fence. Christian yelled, "Where the hell is Adam?"

Peering through the wire mesh I said, "Calm down. Adam just woke up."

He grabbed the fence and shook it. "I told you, I'm not leaving here without Adam. We have to leave today!"

"It's not that easy. Adam and Emma don't wanna leave here. We discussed it last night."

"Bring Adam here, right now! I wanna talk to him."

Looking directly into his eyes, I softly told him, "My friend, that's not gonna happen."

Christian let out a yell and shook the fence like a mad man. Now I knew he was just another bully trying to get his way through intimidation.

"Jack, I'm warning you! I'll release fire and brimstone on you."

"Is that a threat?" I calmly asked, as I pulled out a smoke.

"It's a promise. If you don't bring Adam here in 15 minutes then we're going to have trouble."

"Look, I'm trying to reason with you. Your father wanted it this way. According to him, so did God. Besides, the

kids are safe here."

Christian replied, "Here's what I suggest. You keep Emma, and Adam comes with me. Does that sound fair?"

I laughed in his face. "Christian, I know what you want. So cut the bullshit. If you think I'd let Adam and the sword go with you then you're crazy."

Christian grabbed the fence again and shook it like a crazed gorilla. "You're really pissing me off, Jack! If I get my hands on you, you're dead meat. Open the damn gate! Come out and fight me like a man. No weapons, just good old hand-to-hand combat."

Blowing a white cloud of smoke in his face, he backed away from the fence and coughed. I asked, "Why in the hell should I fight you?"

"You're a coward, a chicken shit. You know I could beat your ass."

"You just don't get it. This isn't about you and me. It's about the kids and perhaps the future of mankind."

Christian's men were gathering behind him. They had their weapons in low ready position. They could kill me and maybe some of my men before they died.

I was trying to buy some time until my men were all in position, at noon, to spring my trap. It was only 11:20 so I had to stall him as long as possible.

Christian asked, "What do you mean the future of mankind?"

"The way I see it, if you get hold of the treasure, then the future of mankind is at risk."

"How do you know about the treasure?"

"Adam told me everything, including the fact that you

tried to steal the sword and kill your brother. That's why you were outcast from the Knights Templar."

"That's a damn lie! He was killed by someone during a home break-in."

One of his men walked up and asked Christian, "Is that true?"

"Yeah, he was killed when someone broke into his house, so shut the hell up."

I replied to the solider, "That's not what Adam told me. Christian tried to steal the sword."

I heard a commotion behind me and turned to see Adam walking towards us wearing a white mantle with the crimson cross on it. The Sword of Jerusalem was strapped on his waist.

I asked Adam, "What are you doing?" He looked at me but didn't reply.

Adam walked up to the fence peering at Christian. "I'll give you the sword under the condition that Emma and I stay here."

Big Christian thought about it for a minute. "It's a deal, if you tell me what the sword says."

"Ok, I agree." Adam replied.

I said, "Adam, wait don't agree to that."

"I have to. Please open the gate."

I hesitated but nodded ok. Slowly I unlocked the gate and pushed it open. Adam stepped outside with me by his side. I flicked the safety off my M4 as we walked out into the danger zone. I was prepared to kill Christian on the spot.

Adam walked by Christian and stepped up onto a foot high rock next to him. Christian and his men were watching his every move. Gazing at the Templar Warriors, he shouted in a firm voice, "My name is Adam de Molay! I'm the rightful heir to be the next Grand Master!"

In one swift movement, he pulled the sword out of its scabbard, kissed the golden handle, and pointed it at the sky. Holding the blade high in the air, Adam shouted, "This is the Sword of Jerusalem! It holds the secrets to God's Treasure!"

The blade was glowing in the bright sun. It reflected the sunlight like a mirror. Christian's soldiers all dropped to one knee. One warrior shouted, "Praise God!" They all repeated the words in unison and bowed their heads.

Christian saw his men all drop to one knee and so did he, right in front of Adam, a couple of feet away. With Christian's head slightly bowed I saw the sword reflect the sunlight over him.

Quickly and unexpectedly the sword flashed a white blinding light as if it was hit by a lightning bolt. A strong gust of wind blew up at the same time. The odd thing was, there was no noise. It was dead silent. I had to glance away and close my eyes from the intense flash of light. It was so strong; I could only see white spots for a second or two as I was blinded by the brilliant flash.

Opening my eyes, I looked up at Adam holding the sword high in the air. Blood was running down the blade. I realized what had just happened when I noticed Christian's head on the ground. His body, slumped over, was pumping blood out of his open neck.

Adam was still pointing the sword at the sky as crimson red ran down the shimmering blade, and he said, "Glory to God in the highest."

The soldiers keenly looked at Adam and all repeated, "Glory to God." Then they all stood and bowed to him.

I wondered what just happened. Was that an act of God? Did God move Adam's arm to behead Christian? Was God actually using the sword to protect his treasure? Did Adam plan this all along? Supernatural forces were at work for sure.

Adam kissed the handle, wiped the blood off on his white robe, and sheathed the blade. As Adam stepped down from the rock, he slumped to the ground. I jumped to help him back on his feet. He looked dazed and confused.

I kept an eye on Christian's men, not knowing what they would do. Then one man stepped forward towards Adam. Swiftly, I pointed my M4 at him.

Holding his hands up he stopped and said, "Have no fear. My name is Captain George Baldwin, leader of these new Templar Warriors. We're at your command, Adam de Molay. You have just proven that you're the real Grand Master. The law states: 'Whoever controls the sword shall be the Grand Master.' We vow to follow your orders."

The warriors were dressed in all black, SWAT type, combat gear. Baldwin himself was a compelling figure; standing at a little over six feet tall. You could tell he was in the best of shape by the way he moved and stood. One thing made him stand out which was an ugly scare that ran down the entire length of his left cheek.

Now I knew things would never be the same. Adam had become Grand Master by the Power of the Sword. Now he had his own warriors to do God's work.

Adam said, "Thank you Captain Baldwin. I'll need

your help and support."

I stepped up and shook Baldwin's hand. "I'm Jack Gunn, Director of Security for Tocabaga."

"It's a pleasure to meet you," George replied.

I said, "Since Adam is under my protection, I need to know your intentions."

"I understand your concern. We're Templar Warriors who do God's work. It was clear to us that God terminated Christian by working his will through Adam. There is no doubt that Adam has the Power of the Sword and God is on his side.

"As for my men, we were all once Marines before becoming enlightened by God. Most of us saw combat in the middle-east fighting ISIS. After that we decided to do the Lord's work and became his warriors."

Knowing that Captain Baldwin was the commander of twenty-three combat hardened retired Marines made me feel more at ease.

"Captain, Jack Gunn is my guardian, and you will receive your orders from him and me," Adam advised.

Baldwin nodded his head. "I understand."

Tommy, my son, came running over and saw Christian's head on the ground. "Holy crap! What happened?" he asked.

I replied, "I don't know. Get some men over here and remove the body."

Tommy had a puzzled look on his face. He then signaled for a few men to remove the body. As they picked up the body Adam said, "May God bless his soul."

"Captain, please wait here with your men while I talk

to Adam," I said.

I put my arm around Adam and we walked up the bridge. I asked, "What just happened?"

Adam stopped walking and faced me. "God told me in a dream to take Christian the sword. He told me how to hold it. God told me not to fear for my life because he would protect me. When the bright light hit the sword, I lost control of my body. I don't even know what happened."

"Adam, that's incredible. I've seen a lot of stuff in my life, but never anything like that."

"Yes, it was a miracle," Adam said.

That's what happened on September 14, 2025 when young Adam de Molay became the new Knights Templar Grand Master.

THE SWORD OF JERUSALEM

APRIL 20, 2026

There was a lot of work to do before leaving on the Quest. Using the ACWWW, the Army Command World Wide Web, I found out that the summer solstice would occur on June 21st which left us two months to find the correct location to be in, when the sun rose on that day. One of the clues on the sword stated; *at the head of the trail, leading into the fissure, look for the cross and the Solstice Sun will light the way.*

That meant we had to be at a certain location when the solstice occurred or we would miss the sun lighting the way. We would have to leave tomorrow, if possible. The twenty-four new Templar Warriors, Maggie, and I were working feverishly to make ready for our journey.

We had no idea where the treasure was actually hidden, but only the clues from the Sword of Jerusalem. Over the past six months I had studied the clues and had a general idea, or should I say a guess, of where the treasure could be located.

Now you're wondering: What is 'The Sword of Jerusalem'? Why is it so important?

I first found out about the sword on August 3, 2025. Adam's grandfather gave it to him before he died. I had no idea what the sword was really for or how important it was. I had no idea it was blessed by God and was a powerful weapon in the right hands. If it got into the wrong hands, no one knows what could happen. The following is the true story about the Sword of Jerusalem.

On September 13, 2025, the day before the sword killed Christian, Adam took me to his bedroom to show me the secret sword. I had never seen it close up, out of its box. After walking in the room, he closed and locked the door. He said, "What I'm about to show you is the most amazing secret you'll ever see. Only a few people know about this."

I said, "Don't worry; your secret is safe with me."

Adam stood there next to his bed and took a deep breath. "Ok."

He reached under his mattress and pulled out a wooden box. Opening the box he took out the old broadsword. The scabbard looked old. The handle or grip was inlaid with gold and contained embedded rubies. The pummel had a golden cross on it. Holding the sword in both hands, he kissed the handle and then pulled the big blade out of its scabbard.

"This is the Sword of Jerusalem." Adam said.

It was a beautiful looking weapon. The long blade almost glowed as he held it up in the air. It was shiny and looked like new. I was amazed by what I saw. Adam gently laid the sword on the bed.

"Here, look at this," Adam said, while pointing at the sword. "But don't touch the blade. The rubies in the handle are a symbol for the blood of Christ."

I bent over and closely observed the blade. Some kind of foreign writing was etched in the metal blade. "What does it say?" I asked.

Adam didn't reply. He turned the sword over, showing the opposite side. There was more writing and a map etched into the metal. Adam said, "This is why Christian really wants this sword."

The map was so tiny I couldn't make it out with my bad eyesight. I didn't know the language it was written in. "Ok, I give up. What does it mean?" I asked.

Adam turned the sword back over to show me the text. "This writing lists all the items in the Templar Treasure." Turning the blade back over, he pointed at the map. "This map shows the location of the treasure."

I asked, "Do you mean the treasure items taken from Jerusalem?"

"Yes. I told you before, these are holy items. These items were once in the Temple of Solomon. They prove there is a God and there was a Christ. Men have killed each other for a thousand years to find this treasure."

"Holy crap." That was all I could mutter while

glaring at the magnificent sword.

It was amazing. Now I knew the treasure was real, according to the sword and Adam. I commented, "Let me get this straight. If you have this sword, then you can find the treasure."

"That's correct. This is why we can't let Christian obtain this sword. No evil man should be in control of God's Treasure. I fear my uncle would use it to gain power and wealth."

"Why do you think he'd do that?"

"Well, Grandfather told me that Christian was outcast from the Knights Templar years ago because he tried to steal the sword. Grandfather also believed that Christian killed my father so he could become the next Grand Master in order to obtain the sword."

I nodded my head and thought, this thing has turned into a very big and dangerous mess.

I said, "If that's true then we certainly can't let your uncle take custody of you."

"It's true, alright. Grandpa would never let Christian near us."

"Didn't you tell me you saw the treasure once?"

"Actually, I've never seen it, but I know it's real because of this sword."

I pointed at the sword. "Can you read this writing?"

"Yes, I know exactly what it says. Grandpa taught me. He could read the ancient Latin writing."

A light went off in my head. "Now I get it. Christian needs you to tell him what the sword says."

"Yes, I think you're correct," Adam said. "What are

we going to do?"

I didn't reply right away. I had to think about this. Certainly, if this whole story is true then I can't let Christian obtain the sword, or Adam. The question is, if I don't give him what he wants, then what will he do?

Adam was looking at the sword as I put my hand on his shoulder. "Don't worry, Adam. I'm not gonna let Christian take you or the sword. I promise you that."

Adam gave me a hug. "Thank you, Grandpa." We hugged each other and chills ran down my spine. Goosebumps popped up on my skin as I thought about the Power of the Sword and the secrets it held.

We stood there looking at the blade. Adam said, "You're the only one I can trust, other than Emma. Would you like to know what the writing means?"

I thought for a minute. "Only tell me if you really want to."

"I have to tell someone who's trustworthy, just in case something happens to me."

We bent over the sword. Pointing at the words he said, "This Sword is gifted to the Knights Templar Grand Master by Baldwin the Second, King of Jerusalem. Year of our Lord 1120 A.D."

"That's incredible," I murmured.

"The treasure contains: One hundred thousand gold coins, fifty thousand silver coins, five hundred golden goblets, one thousand silver goblets, twenty thousand pieces of gold and silver jewelry, ten thousand various pieces of art, and twenty thousand gold crosses."

"Is that all it says?" I asked.

"No. It also says the Holy Lance, the Sangreal, and the Ark of the Covenant are part of the treasure. There's a date … 1124 A.D., Year of Our Lord."

I touched Adam on the arm. "If this is real and the Ark of the Covenant is part of the treasure, that's amazing. No one knows what type of power the Ark has. I wonder if the Ten Commandment tablets are inside."

"It doesn't say what's inside the Ark."

"The main story about the Ark is that when Jerusalem was invaded it was taken to Ethiopia. No one has seen it since. Does the writing mention that?" I asked.

"No, it only lists the treasure items." Adam flipped the sword over. "Now, let me show you the map. It also gives clues as to the location because the map is not very telling."

I pulled out my reading glasses and looked at the blade. There was a map that showed a river and what looked like some mountains. There was a hooked 'X' marking the treasure location.

Adam began to tell me a story about the Templars' history.

"The Knights Templar were founded in 1118 by Hughes de Payen. This occurred after they had a meeting with King Baldwin II, the King of Jerusalem. His older brother was Godfroi de Bouillon who led the crusaders to victory in the Holy Land twenty years earlier.

"The Knights offered themselves as an order that would protect the roadways for pilgrims journeying to Jerusalem. They were given an entire wing of the royal palace for their headquarters. The wing had been built upon the foundations of Solomon's Temple. They received their name 'The Knights of

the Temple.' Their real mission was to excavate the tunnels under Solomon's Temple looking for the treasure.

"In 1129, the Roman Catholic Church endorsed them as Holy Warriors and the protectors of Christendom. The Templars' reputation for bravery was well known. They were not allowed to retreat from battle and were obliged to fight to the death. They were also pledged to secrecy about the workings of the order."

"That's very interesting, Adam."

"Oh, there's a lot more, but I'll tell you later."

"Now, tell me about this map?"

Adam stared at the sword. "I'll explain the clues as best as I can.

"Upon arriving at the new land, sail south along the coast. Follow the coast which turns north, where the water is warm. Sail north, along the coast until you reach a great river that flows from the north.

"Sail up the great river for three days. Land at the point on the west bank marked by a stone cross where another great river mergers. The cross will point the way.

"Proceed west on the cross marked native trail for 40 days until reaching the stone trees. Beware of hostile natives along the way.

"Follow the cross west for another eight days to the rock castle.

"Go north for 15 days on the marked trail to a fissure in the earth. Here at the head of the trail, leading into the fissure, look for the cross and the Solstice Sun will light the way.

"It's signed by Jacques de Molay, Grand Master

1306."

I said, "This means the Templars came here in the 1300's which was before Columbus."

"Columbus was actually searching for the treasure," Adam replied. "Do you have any idea where the treasure might be hidden based on this map and clues?"

"No. I though you knew where it was," I said.

"Grandpa tried to find it over the years, but he never did."

I advised, "We need a real map to see if we can determine what these clues mean. Back in those days the country was crisscrossed with Indian trails. The American Indians traveled by foot and took the most direct path. It appears that the Knights used the Indian paths. Many of our modern highways followed those trails."

"Yeah, that makes a lot of sense," Adam replied.

"I think that's enough for today, it's getting late. We'll work more on this tomorrow."

I was really interested in cracking the clues to find the treasure location. Actually going there to find it would be another problem, but the thought did intrigue me.

ANALYSIS OF THE SWORD CLUES
APRIL 21, 2026

Now I have a small army getting ready to follow the clues on the sword. The first clue stated: '*Upon arriving at the new land, sail south along the coast. Follow the coast which turns north, where the water is warm. Sail north, along the coast until you reach a great river that flows from the north.*'

I had done a lot of research and came to the conclusion that the Templars sailed from England, using a Viking map. They traveled south down the east coast of the United States. Then they sailed around the Florida peninsula, where the water is warm, into the Gulf of Mexico. Following the Florida coast north, they sailed to the great river that flows from the north, which has to be the Mississippi River.

The second clue states: 'Proceed *up the great river for three days. Land at the point on the west bank, marked by a stone cross, where another great river merges. The cross will point the way.'*

The problem is there are two large rivers that enter or merge with the Mississippi. They are the Red River and the Arkansas River. Either one of these could be a three day sail from the mouth of the Mississippi. We will have to look for the cross that points the way, but I doubt that after seven hundred years we'd be able to find any sign of a cross.

Clue three advises: '*Proceed west on the cross marked native trail for 40 days until reaching the stone trees. Beware of hostile natives along the way.'*

I found an old army trail map from 1860 on the ACWWW that showed only one trail that heads almost due west. I overlaid this map with a river map and a modern highway map. The interested thing was that the Red River and the Canadian River, which turns into the Arkansas River, both flow from the Amarillo Texas area.

The maps all converge in the Texas panhandle near Amarillo. This meant that the Templars basically followed a trail near the Red River until it ended and picked up another trail heading almost due west. Or they followed the Arkansas River and then the Canadian River to the same area. Indian trails did follow rivers whenever possible because it made passage easier and it provided a source of water.

In any case, it didn't matter what river they followed, if any. The key location was Amarillo, because the old Army trail and modern highway I-40 both went through Amarillo.

Highway I-40 clearly followed the old Army trail. It was almost an exact match when I overlaid the two. There was another important part of the clue. It was the comment: *'Beware of hostile natives along the way.'*

In those days the most hostile natives in that area were the Comanche Indians. They controlled most of Texas including the panhandle up into Oklahoma. The Knights Templar certainly would have run into these natives who were the 'Lords of the Southern Plains.'

The Comanche Indians were feared by all the other tribes because of their fighting ability and fierceness. These warriors killed most people who trespassed into their territory. They took no prisoners except for children and women whom they made into contributing tribal members over the years.

The Comanche territory, at that time, was the prime feeding area for the American Bison. So they defended this area to the death. I have read stories about them painting their faces black and red to scare their enemies when they went to war. When going to war they always outnumbered the opposing force by a considerable amount, to assure victory.

If you were taken alive you could be tortured to death. They considered anyone who surrendered to be coward. Torture at the hands of the Comanche meant a long painful death. Some took pleasure in slowly burning people to death or using them for target practice. Putting as many as 200 arrows into one's body, they tried not to kill you. They wanted to keep you alive as long as possible. Times were different then and they did what had to be done to keep their lands.

The last great Chief of the Comanche Tribe was Quanah Parker. Quanah was half Comanche and English-American. His mother was Cynthia Ann Parker, a daughter of a Texas farmer. Cynthia was kidnapped at nine-years-old and was more or less adopted by the Chief of the tribe.

When she was older, a Chief named Peta Nocona married Cynthia and Quanah was born. He took the name Quanah Parker out of respect for his mother. He once boasted that he had killed more white-men than any other Indian. Quanah Parker was the last in his tribe to surrender to the United States Government and settle on a reservation. He never signed a peace treaty, but he vowed never to fight again. Since he was a respected leader, his word was good enough for all to believe. Quanah Parker was truly a great Native American.

Knowing these tidbits about the Comanche Indians, I now assumed that we were on the right track. During our trip we could stop and visit the Comanche Nation located in Lawton, Oklahoma. Who knows, we might find some clue or information about the Templars. Even if the Indians didn't keep any written records, they did keep a detailed verbal history of important events.

Reviewing clue three again, '*Proceed west on the cross marked native trail for 40 days until reaching the stone trees. Beware of hostile natives along the way.*' The other parts of this clue, however, need to be taken into account. Proceed west for 40 days until reaching the stone trees.

I pulled out a modern road map, as Adam sat down next to me, to study it. Adam asked, "If you travel for 40 days, how far would you get?"

I replied, "If they walked at five miles per hour for ten hours, then that's 50 miles a day. Fifty times 40 days is 2,000 miles. But I doubt they could make that kind of speed back then on the old trails. They had to have horses to carry the treasure and equipment. So I guess maybe about 1,200 to 1,500 miles is more like it."

"It says, 40 days to the stone trees. What are the stone trees?"

"I have an idea. Adam, mark off 1,200 miles, heading due west, on the map from where the Arkansas River merges with the Mississippi."

Adam did the mileage check. "Look, it puts us near the border of Arizona and New Mexico."

I scratched my chin and pulled out a thinking stick – my term for a smoke. I dangled it from my mouth, but didn't light it. Gazing at the map I said, "Eureka! The stone trees have to be the Petrified Forest, located just inside Arizona, off of I-40."

"What's the Petrified Forest?"

"I've been there a couple of times. The trees are so old, they turned to stone. That's the stone trees they're talking about. Those petrified trees are thousands of years old. The stone trees had to be there when the Templars came here."

"Good job, Grandpa."

"Well at least we're reasonably sure that the Petrified Forest is the place to start our search. It's a long way from here. Tomorrow we'll tell the Templar Warriors where we're going."

Adam is now thirteen years old and is brighter than most kids his age. He is very well spoken and has a commanding air about him. At this age he just lacks experience and a general knowledge of life. Adam has a good heart and at one time wanted to be a Minister. Being tall for his age, Adam stands almost five foot ten inches tall, so you would think he was older than he really is. He is a natural born leader, in my opinion.

FINAL DAY ON TOCABAGA APRIL 22, 2025

I had wanted to leave on April 21st but there was still a lot of prepping to do. Mainly we had to load up the trucks and double check all our gear and supplies.

Days before, we had all of the trucks inspected and fixed by our mechanics. They provided extra parts for anything that might break from wear and tear, including extra tires.

We painted all the vehicles Army brown with black camo stripes, placed randomly, to break up the silhouette. We were taking four diesel Humvees. Each had a fifty caliber machine gun. We also had five pickup trucks; four of them were F-250's and one big F-350 diesel powered truck which would be used to pull a trailer.

Going on this adventure were the 24 Templar

Warriors, which included Captain George Baldwin. Of course, Adam and I were going along with Maggie, who volunteered. We would bring our two best guard dogs, Adolf and Freda, making a total of 28 living beings.

This trip might possibly take as long as three months. We could carry enough food and equipment, but the major problem was fuel to run the trucks. We could never carry enough fuel.

This was a 3,000 mile journey and we would need at least 1,800 gallons of fuel. To complicate the matter, five trucks had diesel motors and the four F-250's were gas operated.

To help solve this problem, we out fitted the five pickups with an extra 100 gallon tank in the bed. We also rigged a 200 gallon tank in the trailer for diesel fuel. We were far short of what was needed, but I figured somehow we'd find the necessary fuel along the way.

It was easy to figure out how much food and water was required. Food was two MRE's per day, per man, and dog. That's 56 meals per day times 90 days, or 5,040 bags. We didn't worry about water because we could filter if necessary. However, we would carry 100 gallons of fresh water just in case we might need it when we get to the deserts of New Mexico and Arizona.

Each man would take care of their own equipment such as: Clothing, rifles, hand-guns, and ammunition. Everyone would bring 3,000 rounds for their M4's and M249's, along with 500 rounds for pistols. The M2 machine guns were also pegged to have 3,000 rounds each. Everyone packed rain gear and cold weather clothes.

We divided up all the gear evenly between each vehicle and loaded up. I didn't want all the food, water, or ammo in one truck in case it was destroyed for some reason. Stranger things have happened.

Captain Baldwin and I had a meeting to discuss the route we would take. We sat down to review the map and Baldwin asked, "What's the plan?"

Pointing at the map I said, "Well, our first stop is gonna be the Comanche Nation, near Lawton, Oklahoma."

"I was wondering if you figured out where the treasure actually is."

"So far, not exactly, but we have determined that one of the clues is the Petrified Forest in Arizona. We're heading there after we visit the Comanches."

"Why are we stopping to see the Indians?"

"They might know something about the treasure, because the Templars had to pass through Comanche territory to reach the Petrified Forest. The Indians were the only ones living there in those days. They didn't have a written language, but maybe some type of verbal history was passed down."

Baldwin shrugged his shoulders. "Ok, if you say so. That was a long time ago."

"Yeah, it was a long time ago, but I think it's worth checking out. Once we reach the stone trees, hopefully it will lead us to the next location."

"After all this time, you still don't know the location of the treasure. I hope we aren't wasting our time going on this trip."

Peering into Baldwin's eyes I said, "George, if I thought that, I wouldn't be going on this quest. Do you think I wanna put all our lives in danger for nothing?"

"Ok, I believe you. I wanna find the treasure as much as you do. So what route will we take?"

"I think we need to stay away from the big cities, which usually spell trouble. For the most part we'll stay on the Interstate Routes, but when we come to a big city we'll bypass it and take another route."

"Yeah, I agree with that."

"Here, I've marked it out on this map. We take I-75 to I-10. This part should be clear sailing. Once we pass Mobile Alabama, we pick up Route 49 and take it Route 82. Route 82 keeps us away from most of the big cities. Then we pick up Route 281. That leads us right into Lawton and the Comanche Nation."

"Yeah, I'm with you so far," Baldwin commented.

"Leaving the Nation we take I-40 all the way to the stone trees. There's only one large city we have to go through and that's Amarillo."

"Give me your best guess where the treasure

is hidden."

"To tell you the truth, I'm not a hundred percent sure. But if we find the Rock Castle, then I'll know for sure."

"Alright, I believe you." Baldwin said.

"Do you have any suggestions for the convoy formation?" I asked.

"That's easy. Two Humvees will lead the convoy and two in the rear. Trucks will be spaced a hundred feet apart. The first Hummer will be a scout vehicle and stay ahead of the group by at least a mile."

"Yeah, that sounds good. Anything else?"

"We'll stop for the night, while it's still daylight, and make a secure camp. That way we'll know what's around us."

"Ok, then you select the time and locations when we stop each day," I advised.

"Ok good, because it's not that easy. We'll need to pick a spot that we can defend and one that allows us an escape route. I'll ride in the scout truck because I have a good nose for detecting an ambush. We'll scout the camp locations ahead of time to make sure they're safe."

"How many miles a day can we make?"

"If we keep our max speed to 45 mph then the Humvees have a 300 mile range. We'll refuel the trucks when we make camp. That means we'll be on the road for 7 to 8 hours a day."

"Anything else?" I asked.

"No, not right now. Give me a copy of the

map to show my men."

"Take this one."

"If we're leaving tomorrow, what time you wanna roll out?"

"How about 9 am."

George stood up and shook my hand. "See you then, Jack."

I went home to have dinner with my family. As we sat down to my last supper on Tocabaga, everyone was quite. I looked around the tables at each person. "Let's pray," I said. Everyone bowed their heads. "Dear God, tomorrow we go in search of your treasure. Please watch over my family and protect them from evil. Amen." That was it, short and simple.

After dinner, Tommy gave me his Cobb 50 sniper rifle. "Here, take this you may need."

I replied, "Thanks a lot. It might come in handy."

A Cobb 50 caliber rifle fires a big BMG round and can reach out and kill someone a mile away. I call it the superman bullet because it can destroy an engine block. If one of these rounds hits a person it just blows them apart, into big chunks of meat. You're as good as dead.

My wife and I have two children, Tommy and Amy, who are both in their late thirties. Tommy was a Marine Scout Sniper during the Second Korean War in 2018. He'll be in charge of the family while I am gone.

Amy is a RN and takes care of medical needs for anyone on Tocabaga along with Doc. Scott, our only Doctor. Jim Bo, my son-in-law, and Ron, my brother, would also look after the family. They would be well protected.

As I promised, I wouldn't go on this quest if the Army Rangers hadn't returned to Fort Desoto. Last November they returned in full force, so Tocabaga is well protected with 500 Rangers based at Fort Desoto. The Fort is located on the only island which is connected to ours, by a bridge.

My good friend, Captain Sessions, is the commander of the Ranger base and I was sure he would defend Tocabaga to the death with his men. I was ready to depart on this trip with very little concern for the safety of my family and friends on Tocabaga.

The problem was my family would worry about my safety, since I was going into the Wild West. My wife, Hemmi, was really worried and told me in so many words, as we got ready for bed. "Jack Gunn, if you get killed I'll never speak to you again." Then she laughed a little, as tears ran down her face. I tried to reassure her that I'd be fine.

My wife fell asleep wrapped in my arms. I couldn't sleep thinking about leaving her behind. Finally, after laying there for a few hours, I drifted off into dream land.

THE QUEST DEPARTURE DAY APRIL 23, 2026

Hemmi made me breakfast and when I was finished eating she said, "Once you walk out that door, I'm afraid you won't come back. So … don't say good-bye. Just say, I'll see you soon."

Becoming a little teary-eyed, I could only manage to say, "Ok Honey, I'll see you soon." We held each other for a few minutes in a tight squeeze. I kissed her forehead and walked out the door. There were no good-byes. I would try to phone Hemmi using my Army Satellite phone, given to me by Captain Sessions. This was our only way to stay in touch.

Picking up my gear, I walked outside and found Adam waiting next to the truck with Adolf by his side. It was departure time.

Everyone on this adventure would need to be

able to defend themselves. Over the last six months I spent a lot of time training Adam in the use of firearms. He has a good eye and is a dead shot. He knows how to clean and use every weapon except for the M2 machine guns.

Adam was bursting with joy. He was anxious to get going. "Come on Grandpa, hurry up!"

If it wasn't for him and the sword we wouldn't be going anywhere. I suddenly wished I had never seen the sword. It was drawing me away from my family. I had never been away from my wife for more than a few weeks. I had a sick feeling running through my gut.

The convoy was lined up in front of my house. I said, "Adam, ride in the last Humvee." I figured that was the safest vehicle for him to be in if we were attacked.

"But, I wanna ride with you, Grandpa."

"Ok fine, then jump in the back." Adam and Adolf jumped in and he carefully placed the box which contained the Sword of Jerusalem under the back seat, next to my Cobb 50 caliber sniper rifle.

Maggie walked up with her dog Freda. "Can I ride with you, Jack?"

"I thought you'd be riding with Captain Baldwin."

Maggie looked at me and shook her head. "No, we don't have too much in common."

I glanced at her with an inquisitive look. "Oh, I didn't know that. Jump in, you're driving."

We would be driving an F-250 four door. I'd rather ride in this than a bumpy Hummer. Our truck was the third truck in line, behind the first two Hummers. Long ago, the air conditioning had stopped working on all the trucks. It was going to be a hot windy ride with the windows rolled down. Daytime temperatures were running in the mid-eighties, but it was going to become a lot hotter by June. In Arizona June temperatures commonly reach over a hundred. I had been there years ago, when it was one hundred-fifteen degrees.

While standing at the side of my truck, Captain Sessions pulled up next to me. I stepped over his vehicle. He said, "You got everything?"

"Yeah, I think so."

"Well, I think you're in good hands with Captain Baldwin." He stuck his hand out the window for me to shake. "Jack, here's a letter signed by me. If you get stopped at any Military checkpoints, show them this letter. It advises that you're on official Army Ranger business and to let you pass without interference."

We shook hands. "Thanks Captain. It may come in handy."

"I wish I was going with you. Good luck and God's speed. Oh, and don't worry about Tocabaga while you're gone."

"With the Rangers here, I never worry." Sessions drove away just as Baldwin was approaching.

Over the last six months Sessions and

Baldwin had become good friends. Baldwin and I had informed Captain Sessions of our quest to find the lost Templar's Treasure. He was in full agreement with the mission.

Baldwin came down the line of trucks making sure everyone was set to leave. A crowd of people had gathered to see us off. My whole family was outside saying good-bye except for my wife. I understood her feelings, so it didn't bother me that she didn't come outside to send me off.

As I climbed in the truck, Baldwin yelled, "Move out!"

The convoy started to roll. We rumbled over the Tocabaga Bridge as people waved and shouted good luck. I glanced back, over my shoulder, and spotted my wife standing next to my son. He had his arm around her. I saw her wave good-bye.

Adam shouted, "Here we go!"

Maggie and I didn't say a word. We had been off of Tocabaga many times. We knew how dangerous the outside world was. I was happy to have Maggie riding with me. I knew if we got in a bind, she would watch my back. Maggie is not afraid to kill dirt bags, and believe me she has killed a few.

We passed through St. Petersburg and Tampa with no major problems. We were about an hour and a half out, approaching the Bushnell exit on I-75. I clicked my radio and told everyone we're stopping here for a break to visit the grave of Jack de Molay."

Baldwin replied, "I'm gonna scout up ahead,

for a few miles."

Adam's real Grandfather was buried here on the side of the highway. The convoy pulled over and slowly rolled to a stop. There were a few cars and trucks running north and south bound. Most of them went speeding by without stopping or slowing down. A few did slow down to see what the Army convoy was doing. Some of them even waved to us.

Adam, Maggie, and I dismounted with the dogs and crossed the highway to view the grave. The weeds had already grown so high and thick that we could just barely make out the top of the white cross.

It was a bright sunny day with a slight breeze blowing. Adam spoke as he looked at the grave. "Grandpa, we're on the way to find the treasure. If we find it, I'll let you know. Rest in peace." That was all he said.

As we were returning to the truck, I looked down the highway behind us. I could make out a line of cars about half a mile away. Grabbing my binoculars, I zoomed in on them. There were ten vehicles stopped on the roadside. I wondered if they were following us.

Maggie asked, "You see something, Jack?"

Handing her the spy glasses I said, "Here take a look. There's ten cars stopped down the road."

She took a look-see. "It's probably nothing to worry about. They'd be nuts to attack us."

Taking back the binoculars, I took one more glance at the cars. "Yeah, your right, I worry too much." I made a mental note that the first one was a black pickup truck and the next two trucks in line were white. I thought, *I'll keep an eye on them just in case.*

Our convoy continued on with no problems until we reached the intersection of I-10. At this junction we would head west on I-10. Interstate I-10 runs all the way from Jacksonville to Los Angeles. This is the most southern route across the United States. It's the route that illegals take coming from Mexico. Drug gangs, terrorists, and all kinds of dirt bags use this highway.

Baldwin radioed, "Jack, we got an Army checkpoint up ahead. Everyone be alert and tighten up the formation."

I responded, "Are you sure they're really the Army?"

"Yeah, I just pulled up to them. Looks like they're 82nd Air Borne."

At the Interstate junction, Army security was blocking the road. They had a check point set up to help control who was moving around on the Interstate highways. This would probably be the first of many that we might run into.

There were, by my estimate, 30 troopers who were stopping all vehicles heading north, south, east, and west. We slowly came to a stop, behind Baldwin at the checkpoint, following a guard's order.

Glancing around I noted at least twenty cars were being searched or waiting to be searched. There was a small fenced-in area under the bridge, which contained some men apparently being held by the Army.

I watched Baldwin get out of his Hummer so I dismounted, leaving my M4 in the truck, and went to show the guard my letter from Captain Sessions.

The soldiers had shoulder sleeve insignias, indicating they were from the 82nd Air Borne Division, which is based at Fort Bragg, North Carolina. A Sergeant asked Baldwin where we were going. He also wanted to know what we doing with Military Humvees.

The U.S. Special Forces are trying to clean up the crime and terrorist activities. One way to do that is to make it difficult to travel around the country freely. To stop the flow of dirt bags, gangs, and guns one needs to slowly close in on their strong-holds and then eliminate them.

I interceded in the conversation. "Sergeant, my name is Jack Gunn. Please read this letter from Captain Sessions, who is the Army Ranger Commanding Officer at Fort Desoto."

The Sergeant nodded his head and opened the letter. After a few minutes he said, "The letter doesn't state what your mission is or why you have Military equipment."

While we were talking, a few of his guards were walking up and down the road next to our vehicles. I noticed some of our people were taking to the troopers, but I couldn't hear what they were talking about. Most likely they were pumping my men for information.

I advised the Sergeant. "Our mission is classified. As for our equipment, it was provided by the Rangers at Fort Desoto."

"I can't let you pass until I know where you're going and what the hell you're doing."

"Sergeant, please ask your Commanding Officer to come here so we can clear this up. I can get Captain Sessions on the horn, and they can discuss it."

The Sergeant sent one of his men to bring their Commanding Officer over. While waiting, the Sergeant said, "Man, you guys are loaded for bear. It looks like you're going on a long trip."

I pulled out a smoke, a Winston light, and offered him one. He gladly accepted it and I lit us up. After taking a drag, I replied, "Yeah, we're going to Arizona. That's all I can tell you."

Baldwin was sitting on the bumper of the Hummer not saying a word. He was just taking it all in and letting me handle the situation. Thirty minutes went by and now all of our men had dismounted and were sitting on the side of the road, trying to keep cool.

Maggie and Adam strolled by us walking the dogs, and the troopers stared at her. Our conversation came to an end, as the troopers goggled her swaying body. They apparently hadn't seen a good looking chick in a while.

Finally a Humvee pulled up and a Captain stepped out of the truck. "What seems to be the problem here, Sergeant Whitehead?" I waited for Whitehead to give his story to the Captain. I watched as he handed my letter over to him. The Captain read it. "Which of you is Jack Gunn?"

"I am, Captain."

"I know Captain Sessions, we went to West Point together. How's he doing anyway?"

"He's doing fine, Sir."

"I've never heard of Fort Desoto. Where the hell is that?"

"It's right near the Skyway Bridge, in Tampa Bay."

"The next time you talk to Sessions, give him regards from Captain Jim Jones. Tell him JJ said hello."

"I'll do that, Captain."

"Which direction are you going?"

"We're headed to Arizona."

"Ok Jack, you're free to go. A word of caution, be careful on I-10, it's very dangerous around New Orleans. There are a lot of shitheads still out there."

"Roger that, Captain. Thanks a lot."

We mounted up and the Sergeant let us pass; half raising his hand as if to wave good-bye. As we went up the I-75 exit ramp bridge, to access I-10, I made it a point to peer back down the road. I had a good view for about a mile. I was looking for the cars that I thought were dogging us. I was surprised; there were no cars behind us. I guessed they turned off I-75 and were not on our tail after all.

The radio crackled. "Jack, once we get past Tallahassee, I'm gonna scout up ahead for a place to camp. It's getting late. Looking at the map, a good place might be Falling Waters State Park. You know anything about it?"

"No. But if it has fresh water we can get cleaned up."

"I'll check it out and get back to you."

"Roger," I replied.

Our big off road tires continued rumbling down the highway for another hour and a half. We did see some other cars on the road which presented us no problems. From the checkpoint I counted about 200 cars moving east. We had 35 cars pass us going west. All were in a hurry it seemed, zooming by us at more than 70 mph.

Where these people were going, I had no idea. Perhaps they were trying to find families, friends, or just moving to a safer place. People saw our armored Humvees with the big machine guns and stayed away from us for the most part. So far we haven't had a run-in with any dirt bags.

We've been driving now about eight hours and didn't have any encounters with Free Roamers or anyone. We did see a broken down car on the side of the road every now and then. That could mean that things were getting better, at least in Florida. I wondered what we would find as we proceeded further west.

My radio buzzed. "Heads up, everyone." It was Baldwin. "We just checked out the Falling Waters and it looks like a good place to camp tonight. Exit at Route 77 and head south for a mile. Then follow the signs east for about three miles to the park. Once inside follow the road straight back to the falls and you'll see us near the lake."

"Ok, got it George," I replied. We were an hour behind Captain Baldwin.

While driving Maggie said, "Great there's a lake. I can go swimming and clean up."

"Can I go swimming, Grandpa?" Adam asked.

"We'll see. There could be gators or water Moccasins there."

We were all tired and sweaty. A nice cool dip would really feel good, I thought.

"Stop trying to scare us, Jack," Maggie said.

"I'm not trying to scare anyone. There has to be snakes and gators there."

Exiting I-10 on to Route 77, we drove south to the sign that read, 'Falling Water State Park.' Following the road, which wound thought the dense woods into the camp ground area we could hear the thunder of the waterfalls ahead.

The whole area was beautiful, with thick dense trees of all types. Of course, the jungle had almost covered the old cement road since it had not been maintained in years. Even over the noise of our motors, we could hear birds of all species chirping away.

I noticed two RV's, off the road, parked far back in the woods. Maggie spotted a few people along the way who ducked back into the dense forest when they saw us. Other than that, we saw no one else at the park.

Baldwin's truck was parked near a small lake not far from the waterfall. Pulling up, he directed each vehicle exactly how to park. He arranged the trucks into two parallel lines. One line was made up of the combat Humvees, which were located on the north side. The pickup trucks made up the second line, which parked about 100 feet from the shoreline of the lake. The lake assured us protection from the south. The east and west were all open ground which could be easily protected. The trucks were parked facing the same direction to permit us a fast escape in case we were attacked by an overwhelming force.

We set up camp and refueled the trucks. After that, most of the men went for a swim and washed up, while some of us gathered fire wood. We built small camp fires to heat our meals and boil water.

After eating our delicious MRE's, it was dark so Baldwin posted two guards for the night. Adam went to sleep in the backseat of the truck. Maggie and I dragged two old rotted picnic tables close together for our sleeping arrangements.

Adolf and Freda, who ate their MRE's with no problem, because they smell like dog food, were tied to the tables with a long leash. If anyone or anything came around during the night the dogs would let us known.

As I fell asleep, the frogs and crickets were really making a racket. I heard an owl hoot, over and over. It was like music to my ears. It was a beautiful night to sleep under the stars.

Adolf and Freda's growls woke Maggie and me up. I glanced around and saw the dogs looking at something. Grabbing my flash light, I pointed the beam to the edge of the water. My beam picked up its glowing red eyes. The gator was barely out of the water, coming over for some dog food. It was a big one, about 10 feet long. A big gator like that would make a meal of our dogs, so I put them in the truck, out of danger.

Maggie said, "Damn gators, they'll eat anything. Can they get us on this picnic table?"

"I don't know."

"Well, I'm gonna sleep in the truck with the dogs." Maggie picked her sleeping bag and headed for the truck. "Are you coming?"

"No, I'll stay here. I can't sleep now. It'll be daylight soon." A movement caught my eye. It was the gator slowly moving towards me.

Maggie and I go way back. We're just good friends who trust each other. She volunteered to go on this mission because she likes adventure. She's a damn good fighter and is pretty much fearless. Maggie can drive anything from a truck to a tractor. I recall one time we went to Ellenton to buy a tractor from Farmer Horn. Farmer Horn was a real slimy piece of crap, who lured Maggie there on the pretext that he had a tractor for sale, on the internet. His real intention was to kidnap her. He wanted to use her for breeding stock with his inbred sons. Well to make a long story short there was a gun battle with the Horn clan. It didn't end well for Horn because Maggie shot the big pig in the eye when he grabbed her and wouldn't let her go. That day we probably killed fifteen men from the Horn clan. That's also the day we had a run-in with Federal Agents, who tried to take our guns. It didn't end well for them either, but that's another story.

I screwed the silencer on my M4 so I wouldn't startle our men awake. To kill a gator you need to pop him in the head, right near the ear. One shot there and he's dead. I waited for him to come closer. The big boy was right next to the table I was standing on. I had never been this close to one before. They are frightening prehistoric creatures. While stalking you they don't make any noise, but just keep watching for you to make the wrong move.

He was trying to figure out how to get up to me. His head was three feet away as I aimed and squeezed the trigger. I hated to kill him, but he pressed his luck. With that big monster around we weren't safe. I shined my light around looking for more gators, but didn't see any.

One of the guards heard the pop of my gun and came over to see what was going on. "Everything ok here?" Pete asked.

Pete was second in command under Captain George Baldwin. He was one of the most experienced warriors. The other Templars respect him, and follow every order to the letter. Pete looks like a normal lanky guy, standing over six feet tall, but he's fast and strong. He's a lean mean fighting machine.

"Yeah, I just killed a gator that got too close."

He walked over to it and kicked it. "That's a big one alright."

"Have you seen anything tonight?" I asked.

"There was a truck that came in about an hour ago. That's it."

"Where's it at now?"

"About half a mile down the road, parked under a willow tree."

"Did anyone get out?"

"Yeah, a guy came walking over and asked me what the Army was doing here. I told him we were just camping for the night. He just turned around and left without saying a word. I kept an eye on him until he got back in his truck."

I nodded my head. "You see anyone else?"

"Nope."

"It'll be daylight soon. I'm gonna start a fire and make some breakfast."

"Yeah, it's almost 5 am. I gotta wake up my men."

INDIANOLA
April 24th, 2026

After eating breakfast, I pulled out the map. As I was studying it, Captain Baldwin sat down next to me at the picnic table. "Good morning, Jack. I'd like to get an early start today."

"Morning, George. Yeah, I agree."

Baldwin pointed at the map. "I was looking at the map and found a shortcut. If we pick up Route 98 out of Mobile, it will cut off some time. We can take 98 all the way to Hattiesburg and then pick up Route 49 there. It could save us about two hours."

Once we left Florida our trip would take us through the southern tip of Alabama and across the State of Mississippi, where we would pick up Route 82 right outside of Greenville, at Indianola. Then we would cross the Mississippi River using the bridge on Route 82. I hoped the bridge was still intact. That would take us into Arkansas. We'd drive across the southern part of the state to the little city of Texarkana, located on the border of Texas.

I followed George's finger on the map. He was right, taking Route 98 was a good short cut. "Ok, George that looks good to me. We'll take 98 to Route 49."

We had four cities, of considerable size, to go through which was Mobile, Hattiesburg, Jackson, and Wichita Falls in Texas. There were also a lot of small towns along the way while going through good-old-boy country.

Baldwin said, "I'd like to make it to Greenville today, and cross the Mississippi before dark."

Checking the time it was 6 am and the sun was coming up. "Ok, that sounds like a plan. I'll get Maggie and Adam ready to roll out by 6:30."

"Ok, 6:30 we move out." Baldwin went to advise his men to pack up.

Maggie and Adam were already set to go. As Maggie was getting in the driver's seat I told her, "I'll drive first today. We'll switch every two or three hours."

"Ok, sounds good to me," Maggie replied.

Adam asked, "Can I drive?"

"Maybe, when we're out in the wide open spaces of New Mexico," I told him.

Since Adam was a big kid for his age, and could reach the pedals, I had been teaching him to drive just in case there was a problem. I have to admit, he's a pretty good driver, but needs a lot more experience.

I commented, "Adam, would you mind riding in Pete's Humvee today."

"Ok, if you want me to."

"We're going into unknown territory and if any shooting starts, you'll be safer in the bullet proof Hummer."

"Ok. I think it'll be fun." Adam ran over to Pete's Hummer which was right in front of us. I watched him climb in.

Maggie said, "Well, it's just you and me, Grandpa."

"Yeah, just you, me, and the dogs," I said, with a chuckle.

Our little convoy started to pull out of Water Fall State Park. As we rolled past the willow tree, I looked at the truck parked there. It was a black pickup, just like the one I saw dogging us yesterday. I wasn't sure if it was the same one or not, but my sixth sense told me something wasn't right. I gawked at the driver sitting behind the wheel, but couldn't make out his face because of the dark shadows created by the willow tree.

I said, "Maggie, I think that's the same black truck we saw yesterday."

Maggie leaned over, close to me, putting her hand on my leg to look out my window. "Yeah, it might be the same one."

I pushed her back to her side so I could drive. Maggie gave a giggle because she was teasing me on purpose. "Stay on your side of the truck, hot pants," I joked.

"That was an old Chevy. It had spotlight on the driver's side," Maggie said.

"Good eyes, Maggie. I didn't see the spotlight."

We were back on I-10 as I shifted the truck into high gear reaching our standard cruising speed of 45 mph.

I asked, "Maggie, how come you didn't wanna ride with Baldwin?"

"He's kinda weird. I gave him every chance, if you know what I mean, to start something, but he didn't do anything."

I thought about this for a moment. "Maybe he can't do anything."

"What do you mean?"

"Well, maybe he was injured in combat while fighting ISIS. Maybe he can't do anything."

"That's terrible. I never thought of that."

"Yeah, maybe he can't do anything sexual, for some reason, but just desires having a woman to talk to."

"You might be right. Now I feel bad that I didn't ride with him."

Baldwin came on the radio. "I-10 is clear going through Mobile."

Pete replied, "Roger that, Boss. We're right

behind you."

Mobile looked like a war zone. All along Interstate 10 there were burned up cars and trucks. Every now and then we'd see a body or two on the side of the road. Maggie was keeping her eyes peeled for trouble. I had to watch the road carefully, looking for debris and junk on the road. I was weaving around a lot of metal and glass to keep from getting a flat tire. From the Interstate we observed buildings burning and heard some gun fire in the distance. I wanted to get out of the city as fast as possible.

Suddenly, two cars entered the freeway, from the on ramp, on our right side. One pulled up, within a few feet, next to us. Maggie looked out her window at them. She yelled, "They got guns! They're telling us to pull over!"

"We're not pulling over. Shoot their tires first and then the cars," I told her.

Maggie racked her M4, leaned out the window, and fired a few bursts at the closest car. "I blew out their tires!" she yelled.

"Good shooting."

I looked at the car as it weaved to the right, and then turned towards us. It was going to ram us. I punched the gas while swerving to my left. The car still hit our right-rear fender spinning us slightly sideways to the right. The tires squealed as our truck pitched back to the left. I punched the gas, and counter-steered to keep from losing control. We were on two wheels for a second, and on the verge of rolling over. I held my breath as our truck bounced back onto all four wheels, wobbling back and forth, as we sped away.

Glancing in the mirror, I saw the attacking car roll to the left side of the road, smashing into the concrete barrier, coming to an abrupt stop. The other car followed it going right in between our truck and the truck behind us in the convoy. They just missed colliding with each other. The second attacking car also collided with the barrier and the other car.

The radio crackled and Pete yelled, "Jeff, blast those assholes!"

Jeff was in the last combat Humvee, at the end of the convoy. He's the third in command of the modern Templar Knights. Jeff is a dead shot with any weapon. He's the best shooter with the big fifty gun.

All the vehicles in our convoy had made it past the attacking cars. Pete's brake lights came on and the whole convoy came to a screeching stop. We watched Jeff's machine gun open fire on the cars. Their gas tanks exploded and the cars started on fire. No one escaped the deadly rounds from the fifty caliber machine gun. A few men made it out of the flames; but were easily mowed down. Eliminating those dirt bags was easy work for Jeff. The battle was over in a few minutes. It was amazing how quickly the cars turned into huge fireballs spewing black smoke high in the air.

Sitting there watching the action, my hands and feet started to shake. I have to admit, almost flipping over got my adrenaline going. I lit a smoke to relax.

We continued on our way until reaching Route 98. Captain Baldwin was standing in the road waiting for us. We all needed a break and so did the dogs. Maggie let them out to do their business.

Jeff strolled up to me and shook my hand. "Hey, good driving. I thought for sure you were gonna roll."

"Yeah, it was a close one." We examined the damage done to my truck from the collision. The right-rear fender and quarter panel had a big dent, but it wasn't anything serious.

Baldwin called everyone over to his truck. All the drivers huddled around as he leaned on the hood of his Hummer and glanced around at everyone. "What happened back there?"

Pete replied, "Two cars tried to stop our convoy. Jeff blasted them to hell."

Baldwin nodded his head like it was no big deal and pulled out his map. "Route 98 is gonna be a crude road compared to the Interstate. It's an old country road probably built back in 1920.

"There are a few small towns along the way to Hattiesburg. We'll by-pass Hattiesburg using I-59 and pick up Route 49. I want everyone to stay close, within a few car lengths. That way no vehicles can cut into our convoy, like what just happened. Jeff, since you're the rear guard, don't let anyone pass you. Any questions?"

I asked, “Do you think we’ll make it to the Mississippi today?”

“I don’t think so, but we’ll try. If there’s nothing else, take a ten minute break and then get ready to move out.”

Maggie gave the dogs some water while I handed out oranges from our farm, to those who wanted one. Maggie commented, “I’m glad you were driving back there. That was pretty scary when we almost rolled over.”

“Thanks, Maggie. You drive for a while. I need a break.”

She laughed and punched my arm. “Ok, I’ll drive.”

I saw Pete and Adam talking to each other and sharing a bottle of water. That was a good sign because Adam doesn’t usually spend a lot of time talking to the Warriors. I think he feels intimidated because of his young age. Of course, the Warriors intimidate almost any person.

We made it past Hattiesburg using the bypass and picked up Route 49 taking us into Jackson, Mississippi. We didn’t encounter any problems. Some people we passed, shouted greetings or waved as we drove by. Continuing down Route 49, we reached the small hick town of Indianola, Mississippi. It’s about 30 miles from Greenville and Mississippi River. This is the junction where we pick up Route 82.

A street sign greeted us:

‘WELCOME TO INDIANOLA - HOME

OF BB KING, KING OF THE BLUES'

It was getting dark when we arrived in Indianola, which was a typical small town that reminded me of the old days. On the main drag was one general store, one restaurant, a couple of closed gas stations, two churches, and a bunch of little stores that for the most part were closed. It was pretty much a ghost town. There were a few people walking around who greeted us with a wave. They seemed down-right friendly because they waved and said hello while we slowly drove past them. I had a good feeling about this place. It was peaceful and quaint.

Indianola is located at the junction of U.S. Routes 82 and 49W. The town was originally named "Indian Bayou" in 1882 because the site along the river bank was formerly inhabited by a Choctaw Indians. Between 1882 and 1886, the town's name was changed three times before finally becoming "Indianola," in honor of an Indian princess named "Ola." The town developed and grew at this site due to the location of a lumber mill located on the Indian Bayou.

The city is 8.7 square miles (22 km²) which includes the bayou. Indian Bayou Waterway runs the length of the city and beyond. The topography of Indianola is mostly flat.

Captain Baldwin stopped our convoy in front of the little town square. To my surprise, the American Flag was flying, high on a pole, in the public park. That was a good sign for sure. After we dismounted, George told everyone that it was best to stop here for the night. George posted sentries and had trucks lined up in two rows.

Before we could unpack our gear, an elderly man and woman approached us. I eyed them up right away. They didn't have any weapons that I could see. Just the same, I kept my M4 at low ready position.

"Howdy friends," the man said, as he stuck out his hand.

The man was dressed in a plaid shirt with blue jeans, which were held up with suspenders, and a plantation type straw hat. The lady had on a flowery dress with a sun bonnet, which made her look like an old fashioned country housewife.

Maggie was holding onto our dogs who keenly looked at the strangers, but didn't growl at them. The dogs normally have a sense of who's friendly and who's not.

Maggie and I stepped over to them and we shook hands. "Hello, I'm Jack, and this is Maggie."

The man tipped his hat and he pulled a toothpick out of his mouth. "Hello Maggie, Jack. My name is David Ragsdale, and this here's my wife Alice. I'm the Mayor of Indianola." He spoke in a typical southern accent.

By this time more city people were coming out of the stores. They strolled over to look at our convoy and combat Humvees. "It's a pleasure to meet you Mr. and Mrs. Ragsdale."

"Oh, just call me Mayor, like everybody does."

About thirty people had gathered behind the Mayor, but some just wandered around looking at our trucks. I noticed a few carried shotguns or lever action rifles.

Looking me in the eyes, the Mayor commented, "I don't mean to be nosey, but what brings y'all to our small town?"

"We're just staying for the night, if you don't mind Mayor."

"Heck no, we don't mind. It's great having you Army guys here. We just don't want any trouble."

"We aren't gonna make any trouble. I can promise you that."

Captain Baldwin came moseying over. "Who's this guy?"

"This is David Ragsdale, the Mayor of Indianola, and this is his wife, Alice. Mayor, meet Captain Baldwin the commander of our troops."

"It's a pleasure to meet you, Captain."

Baldwin responded in the same manner. He was going to ask something when Ragsdale interrupted. "If he's the Commander, what are y'all, Jack?"

"I'm the head of this expedition."

"Say, where y'all from, anyway?"

"We're from Tampa, Florida."

Ragsdale stuck the toothpick back in his mouth and nodded his head. "Then y'all are Florida Crackers," he said, with a grin.

Baldwin asked, "Mr. Mayor, do you have any

hostiles around here? You know, people who don't like the military?"

"Of course not. We're all Americans here and loyal to the military."

"That's great. Do you mind if we make a few campfires in your park?"

"Nope, go right ahead."

"Ok, thank you, sir. If you'll excuse me, I gotta tend to my troops." They shook hands and Baldwin left to direct setting up camp.

"Miss Maggie, how about if Alice takes you on a tour of our nice little city," Ragsdale said.

Maggie looked at me. I gave a subtle nod that it was ok. "Alright let's go, Alice," Maggie said. They walked away, arm in arm, like two women going shopping, with the dogs by Maggie's side.

Mayor Ragsdale pulled out a bag of chewing tobacco. Putting a handful into his mouth he said, "Glad she's gone. I needed a chew. My wife don't like chewin' or smokin'." He held the bag out towards me. "Y'all like some?"

"No thanks, Mayor. I got a smoke here." I lit up and we both laughed.

"Hey, where y'all headed to?" Ragsdale let out a big spit and wiped his chin off on his brown stained sleeve.

Taking a drag, I held it in a little while and let the smoke out slowly while replying. "We're … going to … Arizona."

"Arizona. Why y'all going there?"

"We're on a secret mission."

Ragsdale let out another big spit on the ground. "What kinda secret mission?"

I pulled out the letter from Captain Sessions and handed to him. "Here, read this. If I tell you what the mission is, then it wouldn't be a secret."

The Mayor read the letter and gave it back to me. "I see, but can't you give me some kinda hint."

Thinking about this for a minute, I stomped my butt into the ground, putting it out. "Do you believe in God?"

"I'm a born-again Baptist and proud of it."

"That's great, but all I can tell you is we're on a mission for God."

"For God? Now y'all really got me curious."

"Mayor, that's all I can tell you."

"What's all you can tell him?" Baldwin asked, walking up behind me.

I turned to face him. "I just told him we're on a mission for God."

"Yeah, that's right Mayor," Captain Baldwin said.

Ragsdale peered at Baldwin, looking him up and down. "Y'all don't look like normal Army to me. Whatcha carry that big pig-sticker for?"

"You mean this sword." Baldwin touched the handle. "It's to scare our enemies."

"Pray tell me, who are your enemies?"

"Primarily Islamic terrorists like ISIS and al-Qaida. Basically anyone who breaks the law and doesn't honor the Constitution are also our enemies."

Ragsdale nodded his head. "Yep, there's a lot of evil people out there. We're kinda off the beaten path here, so no one bothers us much."

Changing the subject, I asked Ragsdale, "What's up ahead at the Greenville Bridge."

"Y'all planning on going over that bridge are ya?"

"Yeah, we gotta cross the river somehow."

The Mayor spit out some more slimy tobacco laced saliva. He sat down on the bench next to us, as if thinking for a minute. "If you boys are going to the bridge, y'all better be careful."

"Oh, why's that?" Baldwin asked.

"The bridge is guarded by crooks. Bandits that will rob and kill ya. I know many a person that went there and never came back. That's all I can tell y'all."

"So, you've never been there."

"Never been there, and don't wanna go there. Billy Bob went there a few times."

"Who's Billy Bob?" I asked.

"That's my boy. That's him over there by the truck, with the blue shirt on."

"Could we ask him a few questions about the bridge."

"Sure enough." Ragsdale shouted out. "Billy Bob, get over here!"

Billy Bob came jogging over. "What you need, Daddy?" he said, with a smile.

Billy Bob was a big boy, taller than me, but he wasn't a boy. He appeared to be in his early thirties. He dressed just like his Daddy, including the plantation straw hat. He had dark skin, high cheek bones, and black colored eyes, but his hair was light brown.

"Billy Bob, meet Jack, and Captain Baldwin. Billy Bob will answer any questions you got about the Greenville Bridge. I'll see y'all later, I gotta tend to something." Ragsdale slowly strolled away in the direction his wife went.

Baldwin and I shook Billy Bob's big hand. I noticed he had a strong vise-like grip as he unintentionally crushed my hand. I said, "We're gonna cross the bridge tomorrow and wanna know if we can expect any trouble."

Billy said, "Yeah, if you go there it'll be trouble alright."

"Why's that, Billy Bob?" Baldwin asked.

Billy knelt down on one knee and said, "Where's why." He proceeded to draw a crude map on the dirt sidewalk. "Y'all gotta take 82 through Greenville to get to the bridge. It's a bigger city than Indianola is, so you might run into some unfriendly people along the way."

Billy drew the bridge and made a few X's in the dirt. Pointing at the X's he said, "There are usually four guards at a road block. The guards charge a fee to get across the bridge."

"What kinda fee?" I asked.

"I heard about a thousand dollars per car. But I don't know for sure."

"What's on the other side of the bridge?" Baldwin asked.

"I got no idea," Billy Bob replied, while looking at us. "Where are y'all headed to?"

Baldwin and I glanced at each other. We both knew this crossing could be trouble. We had done some research on the Greenville Bridge. It's is a big four-lane bridge. When built in 2010 it was the fourth longest cable-stayed constructed bridge in the United States, running 4.1 miles long.

Baldwin said, "Our next stop is the Comanche Nation, in Lawton, Oklahoma."

Billy Bob touched Baldwin's arm. "Would y'all let me tag along?"

I said, "Sorry Billy, but I don't think so. It could be a dangerous trip."

"Come on, I'll do whatever you want. I gotta get out of this stinking town."

"What about your Mom and Dad?"

"They're driving me crazy. My Daddy is the big boss around here. He's a slave driver making me work my ass off. Always pushing me to get married, and have kids. I don't wanna get married. I wanna see the world."

I stood there not knowing what to say to Billy because he seemed kind of childish. Baldwin asked, "Billy, you know how to use a gun like this?" He held up his M4 in front of Billy's face.

"I never used one like that, but I'm a good shot and a fast learner. I can shoot the eye out of a possum at fifty yards."

"What do you think, Jack?"

Peering into Baldwin's face and then at Billy, I said, "To tell you the truth, you're too green. I don't wanna be responsible for you."

"What if I can help you cross the bridge? Would you let me come along then?"

"How you gonna do that?" Baldwin asked.

"A few of the guards are friends of mine. I could help pave the way. You know, make it easier to get by them."

While I was thinking about his proposal Maggie came jogging up with the dogs. Adolf and Freda went right up to Billy and smelled him. He got down on one knee and both dogs licked his face. Dogs are good judges of a person's character and they sure liked Billy.

I said, "Maggie, this is Billy Bob, the Mayor's son."

Maggie stared at him and said, "Hi, Billy Bob."

Billy stood up, took off his hat, and bowed. "Pleasure to meet you, Ma'am."

"Billy Bob, excuse us for a minute. I need to talk to Jack and George in private." Maggie grabbed us both by the arm, dragging us about twenty feet away.

"Ok, what's up, Maggie?" I asked.

Maggie whispered, "It's here."

"What's here?"

"That black truck, you dummy. I saw it parked on a side street a few blocks away."

"What black truck you talking about?" Baldwin asked.

"I didn't tell you because I wasn't sure, but now I'm sure. Someone has been following us ever since Florida," I replied.

George scratched his chin and was thinking. I could almost see smoke coming out of his ears. "What do you wanna do about it?"

"Nothing, right now. We'll think about it, after we get across the river."

Maggie grabbed me by the arm again. "That's not all I got to tell you. This Mayor and his wife, Alice, are not the nice people they make out to be."

"Oh, how's that?" I asked.

"Well, Alice invited me in their house. While she went upstairs to change her clothes some woman came out of the kitchen. She seemed scared to death and whispered in my ear, leave this town while you're still alive."

Maggie glanced a concerned look at Billy Bob. "I didn't get a chance to ask her why she told me that, because Alice came back downstairs. She saw her talking to me and yelled at her, 'What did you tell my guest?' Then she dragged the woman by the hair into the kitchen. When I heard screaming, I opened the kitchen door and saw the Mayor beating the woman with a cane. Alice and another woman were holding her.

"He saw me and stopped. Then he came after me. Freda and Adolf stopped him from grabbing me. I pointed my gun at him when he drew a pistol out of his pocket. I came real close to killing him. Then I ran back here to tell you guys."

"Did he say anything?" Baldwin asked.

"All he said was, 'Please don't tell anyone. It's all just a mistake.' I didn't stop to listen to any of his bullshit and got the hell out of there."

I said, "Let's ask Billy what's going on?" Maggie and George both nodded in agreement. We moved back over next to Billy, who was petting the dogs. He stood up as we approached. "Billy Bob, what's going on here?"

"Whatcha mean?"

"Tell him, Maggie." I said.

As Maggie repeated her story to Billy, he hung his head down. "I'm ashamed of that. He's a very cruel man. He beats everyone." Billy lifted his shirt and showed us the cane marks on his torso.

Maggie was shocked by the scars on his skin. "Why do you let him hit you like that?"

"If I tell y'all the truth of what's going on you gotta promise take me with you. If you don't, he'll kill me for sure. Y'all promise?"

With hesitation I said, "Ok, you can come with us."

Billy smiled and shook my hand, crushing it

out of joy. "I don't think Ragsdale is my real Daddy. I don't know who my Daddy is, but I don't look like Ragsdale. My mother was a whore who worked for Ragsdale. She was his favorite money maker until she died, a long time ago."

"So what are you telling us?" Baldwin asked.

"Ragsdale owns a bunch of whores and has gambling games. Alice is his Madam who looks after the girls. Ragsdale isn't the real Mayor either. Like I said, he's the Boss Man. This town is under his control." Billy turned his head and scanned his eyes around the park. "You see, only certain people get to carry guns. They work for Ragsdale. You gotta keep an eye on them boys."

"So what does Ragsdale make you do?" I asked.

"I do all his dirty work."

"I take the girls, once a week, to Greenville to make money. That's how I know the guards at the bridge. They always wanna poke my girls. I also collect money from those that owe it from gambling."

"Have you ever killed anyone?" I glared at his face to see if he was telling the truth.

He didn't answer right away. "Yeah, to be honest, I've killed a few bad guys who didn't pay Ragsdale. I had to kill 'em."

I didn't wanna know any details. Most of us have had to kill more than a few bad guys.

Baldwin changed the subject. "Billy, how many gunmen does Ragsdale have?"

Billy Bob counted them out on his fingers. "I guess about twenty guards."

"Here's the big question: Do you think they'll try to attack us tonight?" I asked.

"Well … since Maggie seen Ragsdale doing something bad, he might not cotton to that. Yeah, he might try to take y'all out tonight. He sure would like those trucks and guns, not to mention Maggie."

After telling us about Ragsdale, Billy Bob had gained my full trust.

Maggie said, "I should have shot that asshole."

Baldwin checked the time. "I think they'll attack us when we're asleep, around 2 am. It's 9 pm now. Let's quietly pass the word to get ready to move out. Tell everyone not to make it noticeable. Leave the fires burning, leave some sleeping bags out, and a couple of tents up."

I replied, "Ok, but what's the plan?"

"Everyone be ready to roll out at 11 pm on the dot. The pickups will move out first. The Hummers will provide a rear guard. Once we roll out, head to the bridge." George looked at Billy Bob. "Can we get across the bridge at night?"

"Yeah, I don't see why not," Billy said.

"What will it cost?" I asked.

"Like I told y'all, about a thousand per car."

"Maggie, count out fifteen thousand and give it to Billy to hold. He'll ride with us to the bridge. He'll do the talking and make the payment. We'll cover him in case something goes wrong."

"If something goes wrong we'll blast our way across the bridge. Let the Humvees take the lead across," George commented. Maggie and I nodded in agreement.

"Are we gonna give them the whole fifteen grand?" Billy asked.

"Yes, if we have to," I said. "Billy you stay close to me until we leave. You'll ride in my truck, along with Maggie."

We broke up the meeting and walked around telling our men the plan. The idea was be in your truck and ready to roll out at 11 pm sharp. We noted that Ragsdale had left five men patrolling around our camp at a considerable distance, so not to be conspicuous.

Slowly, one or two at a time, as 11 pm neared our men started mounting up. Maggie, Billy, and the dogs were already in our truck. I was the last one to leave the campsite. After making sure everyone was ready to roll out, I mounted up, started the motor, and gave a hand wave as a signal to move out.

The sudden movement of all our vehicles speeding away at the same time seemed to take the guards by surprise. They just stood there not knowing what to do. Passing close enough by one guard to see the look on his face, I waved at him with a smile. Maggie yelled out the window, "Bye-bye." Billy Bob ducked down in the backseat so he wouldn't be spotted.

Once by the guards Billy sat up and said, "Keep going straight on Route 82 until we reach the bridge. Stop when you see the road block. Then we'll get out and talk to them."

"How far is it to the road block?" I asked.

"It's around thirty miles."

I said, "Maggie, give Billy the money and your handgun."

Before Maggie could reply, Billy said, "She already gave me the money, and I don't want a gun. I never bring a gun with me when I take the girls to visit the guards."

"Ok, suit yourself!" I shouted over the wind noise, while zooming along at 60 mph. "Both of you listen up! When we stop, Billy gets out first. I'll be right behind him. Maggie, you cover our backs."

"Ok Boss," Maggie said.

"Billy, what are you gonna tell these guys?" I asked.

"Good question, Jack. What do you want me to tell them?"

"Just tell them that I am your Uncle Jack. I have nine trucks that need to cross the river. Hand them the entire fifteen grand. Let them count it."

"They might ask why we wanna cross."

"Just say we're going to see relatives in Arizona who need our help."

"Alright, I got it. Don't worry about a thing."

I slowed down to 30 mph so the Humvees could catch up by the time we reached the bridge.

After slowly coming to a stop about 50 yards from the road block, Billy and I climbed out. We approached to within 20 yards and stopped. It was dark and I could barely make out the shapes of the men.

Billy yelled out, "Hey Joe! It's me, Billy Bob!"

Joe replied, "Who's that with you?"

"It's my Uncle Jack. He's ok."

"Alright, come on up here."

Billy and I started walking up the bridge ramp. Scouring around in the darkness I noted four cars were blocking the road. I could only see four guards on duty.

A man walked up out of the shadows and shook Billy's hand. "Joe, how y'all doin'?" Billy said.

Joe had a smile on his face as he replied, "Say, Billy Bob. What's up? Where the whores at?"

"Oh, they'll be here tomorrow. I had to bring my Uncle Jack here tonight. I promised I'd help him get his clan cross the river."

Joe studied me and so did the other three men. "You in the Army?" he asked.

"No, not exactly. We were at one time."

Joe looked at me closer and commented. "Hey Sam, look at this. He's got a real M4 with night optics." Sam came over and stood in front of me, peering at my guns and uniform.

Joe and his men appeared to be just normal good old boys by looking at their clothes and lever action rifles. One man carried a double barrel shotgun. They all had on blue jeans and typical farm boy clothes with cowboy boots.

Sam had on a cowboy hat that he took off to wipe the sweat from his head. Putting it back on, he reached out to touch my M4. I made sure the safety was on while dropping the magazine, took it off the three point sling, and handed to him. "Here, take a look," I said, as I slid my right hand to the grip of my Glock 17, and held it there, just in case he might try something stupid.

He smiled, placed the M4 to his shoulder, and scanned around in the darkness. "Joe, look at this night sight. We need this kinda gun." He handed the gun to Joe for a look-see.

"Yeah, that's sweet alright," Joe said, as he handed the M4 back to me. "Here you go, mister. Can we buy a couple of those guns?"

Billy Bob looked at me wondering what I was gonna say. Joe used the word buy and not the word give, which means he was open to some type of negations. That told me these men were not really cut-throat bad guys.

While ramming the mag back in, I said, "Yeah, I think so. We just wanna get across the river. Billy, give him the money."

I forgot to mention that the money we were using was part of the al-Qaida loot that we captured. Months ago, the Army Rangers and my group of Tocabaga Fighters managed to raid the al-Qaida HQ located near Tocabaga. We found a *million dollars in greenbacks and gold. For killing al-Qaida leaders and taking their funds they put a $200,000 bounty on my head. This led to me being shot in the shoulder by an al-Qaida fighter who managed to infiltrate Tocabaga, but that's also another long story.*

Billy handed him the money. "Here you go, Joe. It's fifteen grand for nine trucks to cross."

"Give me ten grand, four of those M4s, and we'll call it even," Joe said.

I jumped in, "Joe, I'll tell you what. I'll give you the fifteen grand and four guns, if you do us a favor."

"What kinda favor?"

"There're some cars following us. One is a black pickup. It has a spot light on the driver's door. All I ask is don't let it cross the bridge. I'll throw in a case of ammo, too."

"Uncle Jack, you got a deal." Joe was all smiles as he shook hands with me and Billy Bob.

I got on the radio. "George, we just made a deal. Bring four M4s up to me."

"What for? We don't have many spare guns." George replied.

"They're part of the deal to cross the river."

George pulled up in his Hummer with Pete's truck right behind him. When Joe saw our big Humvees with mounted machine guns, I believe he said, "Holy shit."

I walked back to the truck and gathered up

four guns taking them to Joe and his boys. They were like kids at Christmas time. I provided them some basic instructions on how the weapons operated and in fifteen minutes they were set to go. Joe and Sam had some experience with AR15s so they knew the basics.

As we mounted up Joe said, "You know, you coulda blasted your way through our road block."

I just smiled and said, "Yeah, I know, but we don't want any trouble."

"It was a pleasure doing business with y'all," Sam said.

"One more thing. What's on the other side of the bridge?" I asked.

"Maybe a few gangs, but it's nothing you boys can't handle," Joe replied.

As we drove away Billy shouted, "Y'all take care now."

With two Hummers in the lead we proceeded across the Greenville Bridge and the Mississippi. We were now in Arkansas following Route 82, which runs through the southern part of the state. It would allow us to avoid any big cities. Basically, the state has very few cities and towns. From the Greenville Bridge to Texarkana, Texas is almost 200 miles. With any luck we would reach Texarkana by daylight.

Arkansas presented no problems. We didn't see a single person while driving for three hours in the middle of the night. It made me wonder if anyone was alive in sleepy Arkansas.

Baldwin stopped the convoy to refuel and we took a short break. Maggie and Billy Bob let the dogs out. Most of us hadn't had anything to eat or had a chance to clean up from the day before.

I was tried, sweaty, and hungry as heck. I guessed so was everyone else. As I pumped 30 gallons of gas into the tank the fumes made me nauseous. Now I had the smell of gas on my hands which I didn't like. I poured some water in a dish and washed them off along with my face. It wasn't cold but it was wet. It felt good and woke me up a little.

Maggie walked over next to me. "Jack, do me a favor and pour some water over my head."

I laughed, "Really?"

"Yeah, I'm all sweaty and hot as hell."

I climbed into the truck bed, picked up a 5 gallon bottle of water, and turned around to see Maggie had taken her shirt and pants off. Wow, that was a nice surprise. It was dark but there was a full moon and I could clearly see her. She wasn't totally naked, but when I started to pour water on her, the wet underwear left nothing to the imagination.

The other men in our convoy were on the other side of the trucks eating or relaxing. So they missed the show.

Maggie glanced up at me and said, "You like what you see, big boy?"

I stopped pouring the water. "Ok, that's enough hot pants. You should be cooled off by now. How about getting dressed and make us something to eat."

"Ok, party pooper." She blew me a kiss, put on her clothes, went to the back of the truck and pulled out a couple of MRE's. I thought, *damn that little prick teaser.*

We had just finished eating when Captain Baldwin shouted, "Mount up." Everyone scrambled to the trucks. The convoy started to roll. In an hour and a half we would reach Texarkana and the Texas border.

THE TEXAS RANGERS
APRIL 25, 2026

The city of Texarkana is divided in half by the Texas-Arkansas state line. Route 82 passes right through the middle of the city, which used to have a population of around 30,000. Texarkana, Texas is located in Bowie County, named after Jim Bowie who was killed at De Alamo.

We finally reached Texarkana just as the sun was coming up. As we approached the Texas border, there were six police cars sitting there with flashing lights. Slowly rolling to a stop at the road block, Baldwin and I approached ten officers who were armed to the teeth. Our M4's were dangling by their slings and we made it a point not to touch them.

The officers held their guns in a low ready position while watching our every move. One of the officer's stepped forward, closing the gap between us to a few feet. "Howdy boys. I am Captain James Walker. What brings y'all to Texas?"

I noticed he was dressed like a cowboy. He had on a white hat, boots, and blue jeans. I spied the shiny badge pinned to his chest. It was a star in a circle that read in big letters: TEXAS RANGER.

Captain Walker had a weather-beaten face full of premature wrinkles and dark skin which I assumed was a suntan. He stood about my height, in seemingly good shape. I guessed his age to be in the mid-fifties. He just looked like a tough old cowboy. The other men appeared to be in their late twenties.

I replied, "Good morning, Captain. I'm Jack Gunn, and this is George Baldwin. We're just passing through Texas on our way to the Comanche Nation and then to Arizona."

He glanced at our Hummers with machine guns and then peered down the line of our convoy. "Are y'all military people?"

"No sir, but we're working for the Army." I handed him the letter from Captain Sessions.

He read the letter and handed it back. "The letter doesn't state what your business is about. You know, we can't let just anyone into Texas, especially people with fire power like you got."

"We're on a classified mission so I can't tell you any more than that. Like I said, we're just passing through Texas, as fast as possible."

Ranger Walker nodded his head and put his hand on his six-gun, while kinda leaning to one side.

"Where y'all from?"

Baldwin replied, "From Florida, sir. We got all this fire power cause going across country and you don't know what you'll run into. There are still terrorists out there."

"Yep, we know that. That's why we got road blocks up on every major highway. We don't want them coming here and making trouble for Texans."

He stood there for a minute looking at us. I said, "Ranger, do you believe in God?"

"Yes. What's that got to do with anything?"

"I can tell you we're on a mission for God to help save the country."

He looked at me like I was crazy. "A mission for God?"

"Yes, that's right." I pointed at the convoy. "These men are the modern Templar Warriors."

"Templars! I thought they didn't exist anymore."

Baldwin spoke up. "We're the new Templar Knights. We've been going around the country killing Islamic terrorist groups like ISIS, for a couple of years now."

"I see. You men seem on the up and up. Let me talk to my Rangers, cause I got an idea." Ranger Walker went back to the road block and we watched them all huddle together.

After about twenty minutes the Rangers came over to Baldwin and me. Walker said, "We wanna help y'all out, so we'll give you an escort through

Texas to the Comanche Nation. If any other Rangers saw you with those armored vehicles and machine guns, you'd be stopped for sure."

"That sounds good to me," I replied.

Walker said, "It's about 600 miles to the Nation. It's a long drive. We don't want anything to happen to you, so I'll send two cars with you. One will lead the way and another in the rear. No one will mess with you when they see the Texas Rangers in your convoy."

"Top speed of our Hummers is only forty five. That means it'll take thirteen to fifteen hours, not including piss stops and refueling," Baldwin commented.

Walker said, "Anytime you're ready to leave, let me know."

"Ok, just let us top off our fuel tanks and we'll be ready."

"You don't have to worry about fuel in Texas. We got plenty of stations along the way," Walker said.

The famous Texas Rangers have a long and colorful history. By the early 1820s, some 700 families had settled in Texas. There was no regular army to protect the citizens against attacks by native tribes and bandits. In 1823 Stephen Austin organized small informal groups whose duties required them to range over the countryside to help protect the people. They became known as the Texas Rangers. The rangers were paid in property since Austin didn't have the funds in cash to pay them.

However, it wasn't until 1835 that the Texas Rangers were formally recognized. On October 17, 1835 at a consultation of the Provisional Government of Texas, a resolution was passed to establish the Texas Rangers. They totaled 60 men which was distributed into three companies. They were known by their simple uniforms, which were light dusters. The identification badge was formed from a Mexican Peso into the shape of a star in a circle. Within two years, the Rangers force had grown to more than 300 men. The Texas Rangers were known for always getting their man. They were rugged tough men, who risked death almost daily.

We rolled out of Texarkana with Captain Walker in the lead. I was surprised at how normal Texas seemed. People were driving around, stores were open, and life was good. Everywhere I looked I saw a Texas Ranger or the Texas Militiaman. Everyone carried some type of weapon for protection. It was clear to me that there was law and order in Texas.

I was riding with Walker to keep him company and to stay in communication with our convoy using my radio. I asked him, "How many Rangers do you have?"

"No one really knows exactly. Any person, man or woman, who wants to be a Ranger can, as long as their record is clean. All they need to do is get sworn in by the Ranger Captain in their county. Texas has 254 counties and we try to have at least fifty Rangers in each county. Some are more and some are less. Of course, no one gets paid anything, unless you're a Captain like me."

"So to maintain law and order you have the Rangers in each county, sheriffs, local police, and the Texas Militiamen."

"Yep, that's about right. Most Texans want law and order."

Texas has more small towns than Arkansas does. It also has 254 counties which is more than any other state. By my calculations, if Texas has fifty Rangers in each county, then there are 12,700 Rangers state wide. That is a considerable force.

"You seem to have everything under control here in Texas."

"Yep, we don't put up with any bullshit from law breakers. Terrorists we shoot on sight. What about in Florida?"

"We still got a lot of problems, but things are a lot better than six months ago. We have the Army Rangers helping to control the situation. They're slowly bringing law and order back."

"We didn't need the Army to help us here in Texas. I am glad however, that the Army removed the President and the commies from office. How long do you think the Army will run the country?"

"I heard from a good source it may take a while. Maybe years before new elections can be held," I said.

Walker commented, "Who woulda thought, the whole country would go to shit."

"Yeah, almost no one saw it coming."

COMMENTARY ON THE COLLAPSE OF THE GOVERNMENT

The fall of our government didn't happen all at one time. There was no one given moment that signaled the United States was in big trouble. It occurred slowly over a period of years. Like a sandy beach slowly eroding away day by day, as the grains of sand wash away. My best guess is the sand started to erode long ago, in 2001.

Our so-called leaders actually helped make the collapse happen. They destroyed our wonderful country and let the President become a dictator using Executive Order 13603. It was all for greed and power.

Under this Executive Order, everything belongs to the government. Your property, money, guns, and family are being taken. They tell you where to live and work for the betterment of the State. Much to my dismay, we have gone from being the USA to the USSA (United Socialist States of America). It's a downhill spiral that has plunged our country into deep depression, causing even good people to resort to robbery and violence.

Years before, things were not making much sense, especially when the government took control of the news media. It became state owned so the only news we received was what the Federal Government wanted us to see. Back in 2013, the NSA started to tap our phones, read our emails, and our Facebook pages. We were all being watched, we were all suspected of doing something wrong, we were all having our Bill of Rights violated in the name of government security, and no one did anything about it.

Benjamin Franklin once said, "He who sacrifices freedom for security deserves neither."

Unemployment shot up to 55% and everyone knew that things were changing as more and more acts of violence were reported across the nation. Riots, robberies, shootings, explosions, and even attacks on police stations were common. Some states called up the National Guard to help maintain control as desperate people do desperate things. Just driving to the grocery store was becoming dangerous. You needed to carry a gun for safety or your trip to the store could end up being your last.

Our currency became worthless due to inflation and the government closed all the banks to stop bank runs. A loaf of bread went to a $100 and milk to $150 per gallon, if you can find it. People have run out of money and even if they have any in the bank, they can't get it. Savings accounts were wiped out and if you had any gold or silver in the bank forget it, the doors are locked. The government is taking it all because the country is bankrupt.

For many years, illegal aliens have been coming across the border from Mexico. But not all the people are hardworking Mexicans looking for a job. The fact is, many of those crossing the border are from the Middle East and are related to Islamic radical terrorist groups. How do I know this? Because the US Government has admitted that every year several thousand manage to sneak into the USA.

In addition, the gangs and cartels that smuggle dope were also making inroads into the US selling their crap to whatever idiots would buy it. These gangs have turf wars and during their wars they don't care who they rob or kill. Then there is the drug user who robs and kills to get money to pay for his habit. Finally, we have the radical groups, like the Skinheads, Neo-Nazis, al-Qaida, ISIS, and gangs of all sorts. Everyone is trying to take what you have. People will kill you and steal your property. If you are weak, then you will die.

The government is now controlling the food and there are food lines at every store. You must wait for hours to obtain any food. If you can buy food it's only enough for a few days. You can't feed your family on a loaf of bread. Fresh vegetables and fruit cannot be found.

Our once great healthcare system also came under control of the government. Now we have very few doctors to treat the ill. Hospitals have closed and no one wants to work at them because conditions are terrible. The pay is far below standard wage. Basically our healthcare system is no better than that of a third world country.

Can we change what we've become? There's

no country to help us as they've all failed. We're the last hope of free mankind. We cannot forget the Bill of Rights, the US Constitution, and the fact we are One Nation under God.

END OF COMMENTARY

Riding along, on our way to Comanche Nation, it occurred to me that now we know what the American Indians felt like. If anyone got a raw deal it was the Indians. They had their lands and homes taken from them by the government. The government lied to them and broke treaty after treaty. Now we were brothers, so to speak, because we are sharing the same misery brought on by the government.

"I hear tell, that stupid President tried to give Florida to China, to pay the money we owe them. Is that true?" Walker asked.

I replied, "Yeah, that's right. The President was a traitor. We fought off landing parties of Chinese Marines. They had special combat suits which made them invisible. They finally gave up when they lost most of their men trying to gain a foot hold in Florida."

China now holds 55 percent of all U.S. debt. It is the largest holder of all U.S. debt. If the United States cannot repay the debt in an international currency or gold, then China could demand payment in tangible property, such as real estate. The President signed an illegal agreement and gave Florida to China, because they wanted the oil resources.

If you check history, many lands were sold or given as payment of debt. The United States took over Texas, California, Arizona, and New Mexico after the Mexican-American War as payment. We purchased Alaska from Russia. The U.S. purchased land from France in a deal called the Louisiana Purchase. Spain ceded Florida to the United States in 1821.

"If they were Invisible, how did ya kill them?"

"We found out, they weren't that invisible. We could detect them with lasers. Another big factor was their invisible suits weren't air conditioned so they couldn't take the Florida heat. The sun literally cooked them."

Walker gave a chuckle. "Do our Special Forces have anything like that?"

"Yeah. They have Invisible suits and Talos Warrior units."

"What the hell's a Talos Warrior unit?"

"Putting it simply, it's a suit that turns a man into an Iron Man, but he can't fly."

"I'd like to see one of those."

An idea came to life in modern days as a comic book and movie called Iron Man. A man invents a suit of armor and becomes indestructible. In 2011 the Army started a program called TALOS. The Army now has the exoskeleton TALOS combat units that are used from time to time for extremely dangerous missions. These TALOS units have developed into fully armored protective suits that a soldier steps into and becomes Iron man. The only difference is the soldier cannot fly.

Using the most recent model, a soldier can run at 20 miles per hour all day. They can carry heavy items like big 50 caliber machine guns and 500 rounds of ammunition at the same time. They pinpoint the target and fire by eye movement and brain waves. The most important advantage is one can walk through a hail of bullets and not even get a scratch.

A new type of reactive armor has been developed that is more or less painted on top of lightweight thin titanium alloy and beryllium metal, all covered with sheets of Kevlar 10 embedded with a Boron/Silicon Carbide ceramic. The paint is a kind of plastic foam that absorbs energy and behaves like reactive armor. When it is impacted by a high kinetic , it explodes in an outward direction.

Boron/Silicon Carbide ceramic is one of the hardest materials known to man. It has been used to make ballistic armor plates since 1986. Typically, it is used in bulletproof vests as well as tank armor. Upon hitting the ceramic, a bullet will shatter into pieces.

Titanium is recognized for its high strength-to-weight ratio. It is a strong metal with low density. It has a relatively high melting point (more than 3,000 °F). It is non magnetic and has low electrical and thermal conductivity. Some titanium alloys achieve tensile strengths of over 200,000 psi.

Beryllium is a hard metal. The modulus of elasticity is approximately 50% greater than steel. Beryllium is two-thirds the density of aluminum. By weight, Beryllium has six times the specific stiffness of steel and Beryllium is non-magnetic.

Reactive armor is a type of material that reacts in

some way to the impact of a high kinetic projectile to reduce the damage done. The most common type is explosive reactive armor (ERA), but different types include self-limiting explosive reactive armor (SLERA), non-energetic reactive armor (NERA), and non-explosive reactive armor (NxRA). The new foam plastic paint is a combination of all of these types. If damaged in battle, a new coat can be painted on top and it is combat ready in minutes.

The TALOS unit is powered by a small atomic battery pack using a new technology no one has heard of. This power system just popped out of nowhere. These little batteries have over a one year operating life and never need charging. The atomic batteries provide the energy to power the electrical - hydraulic servo systems that make movement possible and super feats of strength.

"Yeah, the Talos Warrior units are really incredible. I've seen them close up. Only the Special Forces use them."

Walker said, "Tell everyone we're stopping up ahead for fuel and food."

It would be a welcomed break since we had been driving three hours already. I got on my radio and advised the convoy as we pulled into a gas station which had a street car diner. The sign above it simply read: 'SALLY's DINER'.

It was a dust-covered little diner out in the middle of nowhere. There were two gas pumps and one for diesel. Behind the diner was a little ranch house.

"Where do you get the gas from?" I asked.

"This is Texas, man. We got no gas shortages here. Let's go in and get some chow. Sally makes the best beef steaks in Texas." Walker replied.

"I haven't had a steak in months."

"We don't have beef shortages either in Texas."

The diner was your typical street car diner from 70 years ago. It wasn't very new, but it was clean. The little mushroom stools at the counter and the seats in the booths were red plastic and every single one had cracks in it from wear. The counter and tabletops definitely showed signs of extreme use.

As we walked in the door Walker yelled, "Sally honey, I brought you some customers."

Sally was a woman in her late thirties with blond hair and a nice figure. She had a real Texas twang to her voice. The dry air and hot sun had taken a toll on her skin, which showed premature wrinkles, but she was still a handsome woman.

Sally ran out from behind the counter and gave Walker a big hug and a peck on the cheek. "Howdy, Captain. What y'all gonna eat." It was clear that Walker and Sally were more than just good friends.

"Round up beef steaks for everyone, with all the fixin's, Sally."

"How many?"

The Captain nudged me and I replied, "We'll need thirty steaks." I included a steak for each dog.

"Wow, that's gonna wipe me out of steaks."

This was going be a long pit stop. All of our men filed in for lunch, filling the little diner. No one talked much because everyone was tired and hungry. When the steaks came out the men gobbled them down, like a starving wolfs. Maggie and Adam took a couple of steaks out to the dogs.

After chowing down the great food, Captain Walker put the whole bill on his tab. I gave Sally a three hundred dollar tip, which she well deserved.

Checking the time, as we pulled away, I noted we spent two hours eating. It was time well spent because my men were tired from being on the road all night. It was a good rest stop giving everyone much needed energy to continue on.

Still riding with Walker, I commented, "Thanks a lot for picking up the tab. That was great food. Good steaks are hard to come by in Florida."

"It's my pleasure to show you some Texas hospitality. Sally makes a great steak and grilled potato dinner. If you don't have beef in Florida, what do y'all eat?"

"We got beef, but not much of it. We mostly eat fish, chicken, and sometimes a pig. We grow our own fruit and vegetables."

"Fish! Damn, I couldn't live on that."

I laughed. "You get use to it when that's all there is."

Walker laughed and said, "Not me. Pig and chicken is ok, but not fish. I can't stand the smell, nor the taste."

I changed the subject. "Captain, are you related to Sam Walker?"

"You know about Texas history?"

"A little bit. I know Sam Walker was the Ranger who helped invent the Walker-Colt pistol."

"Yep, I am related to him. I'm also part Comanche Indian. That's one reason I wanted to come on this trip. I got relatives at the Nation, whom I haven't seen in a while. So I'm kinda curious why y'all are going there."

Now I had to tell Walker why we were going to the Comanche Nation. I couldn't lie about it. Since he was part Comanche, maybe he could help us out.

"Ok, I'll tell you more about our mission. Adam, my adopted grandson, was given an artifact from his real grandfather when he passed away. This artifact gives clues as to where the long lost Templars treasure is hidden. It also tells what's in the treasure."

"What kinda artifact?"

"It's a sword, called the Sword of Jerusalem."

I paused for a minute waiting for a reply from James. "You got my attention. Go ahead."

"The clues are very vague. However, so far I've managed to guess that the Templar Knights brought the treasure to Arizona. On top of that they had to travel through Comanche country."

"What year did this happen?"

"Near as we can tell it was 1300 A.D. when they came here."

Walker said, "I doubt anyone will have information going back that far. They didn't keep written records. But we can ask the Medicine man if he ever heard about the Templars coming through their territory."

"Do you know him?"

"Hell yes, he's my Uncle. He also runs the Comanche Nation Museum."

"That's amazing. We run into you and find the man we need to talk to is your uncle. God must be watching over us."

"Jack, tell me, what's the Templar treasure?"

"It's the lost treasure of King Solomon. We believe it contains the Ark of the Covenant."

"You mean the gold box that contained the Ten Commandments?"

"Well, we're not a hundred percent sure, but the sword says it was part of the treasure."

Captain Walker sat there speechless, just nodding his head as he drove us to Wichita Falls.

I dozed off and not much was said after that exchange. Before I knew it, Captain Walker woke me up. "Pit stop, up ahead."

I rubbed my eyes and sat up wondering how far away we were from the Nation. I picked up my radio and advised everyone we were stopping up ahead.

While refueling, Walker met Billy Bob, and while they shook hands, I noticed that they had similar facical features. In the bright sunlight their skin color was also comparable. They both had high cheek bones and dark eyes. They were about the same size and their posture was high and straight. I studied them and was amazed how much they resembled each other.

We arrived at the Comanche Nation at 8 pm without any incidents. The sun was setting as our trucks rolled to a stop at the gate. Ten armed men greeted us as Walker got out and shook their hands. A few of them gave a typical Indian whoop and yelled 'Tu Puuku.' They all seemed to know him and I stood there watching as they exchanged greetings speaking in their native tongue.

Walker didn't bother to introduce me to any of the guards and told me that we could make camp at an empty lot near his Uncle's house. We got back in his police car and the guards, who all wore cowboy hats with two long strands of braided hair hanging down their backs, waved us past the road block.

While we were setting up camp, Walker said, "I'm gonna talk to my Uncle. Ranger Smith and I will sleep at his house tonight, so we'll see you in the morning. You'll be safe here tonight."

"Ok, whatever you say, Captain."

As Captain Walker and Ranger Smith walked away, Baldwin moseyed over and asked, "Where are they going?"

"They're going to his Uncle's house tonight. He said we'd be safe here."

"Maybe so, but I'm still posting guards."

I nodded my head. "Yeah, I agree."

Everyone was hot, tired, and hungry from the long 15 hour trip. I just wanted to clean up, eat, and hit the hay. Maggie came over and asked, "Where can we get cleaned up at?"

I replied, "I don't have any idea. Where are the dogs?"

"Billy Bob has them over there; doing their business away from everyone." Maggie pointed them out about 100 yards away.

Billy jogged over to us with the dogs. "Jack, there's a motel down the street. Maybe we can get a few rooms for the night."

"Good idea. Maggie, take some money and go over there with Billy. See if you can get twelve rooms for two days. Then we'll be able to take a shower and sleep in a bed."

Maggie said, "That sounds good to me." Billy handed me the dog leashes and they walked towards the motel, a good half mile away.

While they were gone I heated some MREs for the dogs and me. Maggie quickly returned, advising that they were able to get fourteen rooms. She went around and passed out room keys to the Knights.

It was a nice little place called the Comanche Nation Motel. The rooms were plain and the furniture was old. It wasn't a Hilton, but I didn't mind because it was better than sleeping on the ground or in a truck. We'd be doing enough of that on this journey.

All of us took a much needed shower and we felt human again. It's funny how great a shower can feel. The well water had a little sulfur smell to it, but I didn't mind the stink.

I went outside and cracked open a bottle of JD, which I had been saving. I poured a shot and lit up a smoke. Adolf and Freda were sitting at my feet. Driving just poops me out and a shot of whiskey or two would relax me, so I could sleep.

We ended up sleeping in one room with two double beds. Adam and I had one, and Maggie the other. Billy slept on the floor with the dogs.

BLACK HORSE
APRIL, 26, 2026

I heard the rooster crow and opened my eyes. It was still dark, as I glanced at my watch, it was 4 am. That damn rooster wouldn't shut up so I got out of bed, took another shower, and went out for a smoke. I peered down the street at our convoy and decided to walk down there to find some coffee. Passing by the motel office, I saw a person was up and moving about.

Opening the door, I walked in and said, "Good morning."

An old man with long braided grey hair turned around and said, "Howdy Mister. You want some coffee?"

"Yes sir, that sounds great."

He poured me a cup of black mud. "Here ya go. My name is Big Bear."

I stuck out my hand. "Hello Big Bear. Pleased to meet you. I'm Jack Gunn." I put the cup to my lips. The coffee was hot so I slowly sipped it. It had a unique taste. "This is good. What's in it?"

"Oh, a little sage, to add some flavor. It's an old Indian custom."

"I never heard of that before. But it sure is good."

The old Indian took a sip of mud and asked, "So you're friends with Tu Puuku?"

"Sorry, but I don't know anyone named Tu Puuku."

"That's his Indian name. His English name is James Walker."

"Yeah, we're friends."

I pulled out a smoke and offered him one. He took one, looked at it, twirled it around in his fingers, and then smelled it. After that he stuck it between his lips and I lit it for him. "Thanks Mister. It tastes good." I nodded in agreement.

Walker came walking in the door as we were finishing our coffee and smokes. "Hi Jack. Did you sleep here last night?"

"Morning Captain. Yeah, we purchased fourteen rooms."

The old Indian smiled and handed Walker a cup of his sage-laced coffee. "Big Bear, this is still the best damn coffee around."

Big Bear mumbled something in Comanche and the Captain replied back to him. Putting his hand on my shoulder he said, "Jack, you and Billy Bob can speak to my Uncle. He's expecting us after we get some chow."

"Billy don't know anything about what we're looking for."

"I know that, but he wants to meet him for another reason."

"Can I ask why?"

Walker glanced at me. "I think he's part Comanche."

I thought about this for a minute and said, "Now that you mention it, he does appear to have some Indian blood in him. You both have the same facial features."

He let out a little laugh. "You noticed that, did ya?"

Neither of us said another word about the facial similarities.

An hour later, we walked into Black Horse's home. Walker introduced Billy and me to Black Horse. He didn't shake our hands', but just stared at Billy Bob. He didn't say a word for almost ten minutes. He slowly walked around Billy, checking him out from head to toe.

Black Horse appeared to be around sixty years old. His sun-beaten face showed the deep wrinkles of age, but it had a trustworthy appearance. His hair was totally grey with long twin braids which hung to his waist. Black Horse continued to move deliberately around Billy Bob. I liked his half indian/cowboy appearance and calming demeanor. But on the other hand, he was acting kinda weird.

Walker said, "My Uncle's been the Medicine man for 30 years. If anyone knows the history, it's him."

Black Horse was still staring at Billy Bob. He asked him, "What city where you born in?"

Billy replied, "Indianola, sir."

"What was your mother's name?" Black Horse was peering into Billy's eyes.

"Susan, sir."

I could tell Billy was getting nervous and wondered why this man was questioning him so intensely.

Black Horse ordered Billy to take off his shirt. Billy asked, "Why?"

"Just do as I say, boy." Black Horse pointed his finger at Billy Bob. "Hurry it up."

I really wondered what was going on now, but I told Billy, "Go ahead, take it off." Billy removed his shirt.

I noticed a tattoo of a small horse on his right shoulder. It wasn't just any horse, it was a black horse.

The Comanche Medicine man stood up and looked closely at it. He removed his shirt and pointed to a black horse tattoo on his right arm. "I have same tattoo."

"What does it mean?" Billy asked.

"It means you are my Son. Your real name is Little Black Horse. I gave you that tattoo when you were four years old, so I would always be able to identify you."

"You're … my Father? I can't believe it! I found my real Father."

"Welcome home, my Son." They hugged each other and some tears dropped to the floor.

Walker said, "Welcome home, Little Black Horse." They both smiled at each other and shook hands.

Black Horse stepped over to me. "Thank you for bringing my Son to me. I'll always be in your debt."

"You don't owe me anything. It was the work of God," I replied.

Black Horse nodded his head and put his arm around Billy Bob. "Tonight we will celebrate that my Son is here."

In a soft voice Billy asked, "Father, why didn't you come for me in Indianola?"

"Sit down, I will tell you the story."

We sat down, waited as Black Horse lit up a pipe, took a puff, and passed it around the room. "I met your Mother in Indianola one day when I went there to find work. We were young and fell in love right away." He took another puff and thought. "You were born, but we never got married because she was white and I was Comanche. The Mississippi law would not permit it, but you were born anyway. We lived together for four years, until one day a member from my tribe came and told me my Father was sick. I needed to return to the Nation."

He paused for a few minutes, while gazing up at the ceiling, as if he was thinking. "Susan couldn't leave with me because her mother needed someone to take care of her. So we agreed I would go and return when it was possible. You were only four years old when I gave you that tattoo. I remember you didn't even cry."

"Did you ever come back looking for us?" Billy asked.

"Yes, my Son. But it was a long time later. The years flew by and I became the new Medicine Man of the tribe. When I did return your Mother had already died, maybe from a broken heart. I asked many people what happened to her little boy. No one knew what happened to you. After searching for many days, I gave up and returned home. You were always in my heart. I knew that someday we would come together."

"Yes, now we're together. I will never leave your side," Billy said.

"I was loyal to your Mother's memory and never married or had any children. You are my only son."

I sat there speechless because his story brought a tear to my eye. I glanced at Walker and saw him wipe a tear away.

"Father, I feel at home. The empty feeling I had all those years is gone," Billy said, as he touched his father's hand.

"That is good, my Son. My empty feeling is also gone."

Black Horse glanced at me and wiped a tear from his eye. "Now, let's help Jack Gunn with his problem. Tell me what you want to know, Jack Gunn."

I started by showing him a picture of the Templar Cross. "Have you ever seen this shape anywhere?"

Black Horse put on his glasses and studied the picture. "It looks like some kind of cross."

"Yes, it's a Templar Cross."

"I've never seen one before."

"I know the historians and archaeologists say the Comanche Indians didn't live in this part of the country until fifteen-hundred. Is that correct?"

"No. As far as I know my people have lived here since the beginning of time. We have always ruled the plains here."

I said, "Let me explain more. I believe that in thirteen-hundred a large group of men, called the Knights Templar, came through this area from Europe. If I can prove they were here then it would give me the confidence to keep looking for the treasure they brought. Do you remember any history about that?"

"There has been many such people from Spain and Europe coming to our land in the past. We always fight with them because they try to change our ways."

I was getting nowhere fast. I pulled out another picture of a Templar Knight in old battle gear, which showed the shield, helmet, and sword. "Have you ever seen anything like this?"

"Yes. We have many such relics taken from the Spanish Conquistadors. Most of them are in the museum but some are here in my house. Would you like to see them?"

"Yes, please." I thought, *now I am getting somewhere.*

"Ok, follow me." We proceed into a bedroom that was filled with old relics.

The room was dark so I took out my flashlight and shined it around. It was filled with all types of ancient items taken from the battle fields. "May I look around?"

"Yes, of course. There's a lot of old junk here that my people collected over hundreds of years."

I viewed the piles of relics. There were scalps, bows, arrows, and many helmets along with a few shields and some swords. Digging in the piles I found old flintlock rifles and pistols.

Black Horse commented, "Jack, you are the first white man to ever see this collection."

"I am honored to be the first," I said, while still digging.

Black Horse, Billy, and Walker went to sit down while I kept searching in the car size pile of relics. He had a fortune here that any museum would pay money for, when times were good.

After an hour, I had found 12 helmets which were all Spanish, 10 swords, 15 shields, and several old guns. These had to be from the Conquistadors. I walked back into the living room. "I didn't find what I was looking for. Can we go to the Museum?"

"Yes. I will take you now." We walked a few blocks to the Comanche Nation History Museum. It was about 30,000 square feet in size. Black Horse took me to the correct displays showing European relics. There were dozens of metal helmets here and great looking swords with shields. The items on display here were in better shape than the ones in his house.

After another hour, to my dismay, none of the items had a Templar Cross on it. I commented to Black Horse, "Well, that's it. I haven't seen the sign of the cross."

"That's too bad. I really wanted to help you," Black Horse said.

We were walking back to his house and he said, "It just occurred to me that Quanah Iron Coat has some old relics. Do you want to see them?"

"Ok, let's go." We went to Quanah Iron Coat's house, but he wasn't home.

Black Horse commented, "Quanah probably went hunting or is on guard duty. We will talk to him later."

"Is he related to Quanah Parker, the famous Chief?"

"Yes, Quanah Parker is his Great-Great-

Grandfather. But most of us are related in some way to Quanah Parker. It is rumored that he had many wives and children. You can find his life story on the internet."

"Yes, I read about him. He was a great warrior who helped his people."

On the way back, to Black Horse's house we passed by many people. Black Horse made it a point to introduce his son and tell each person the story about finding his son. He told the story with joy and cited me as the person who brought his son to him. He advised everyone there would be a celebration tonight at 9 pm in the town park.

Even before 9 pm, people were gathering in the park. I was the only one invited from our group. Captain Baldwin and his warriors stayed close to the motel and trucks along with Maggie, Adam, and the dogs.

I felt totally out of place, since I couldn't understand Comanche and didn't know the customs. It was a big event and I would guess over a thousand people showed up to pay respects to Black Horse and to meet his son. Black Horse introduced me as the friend who returned his son.

Of course, there was an abundance of food provided by the women, who were continually cooking the beef over wood fires. It seemed like a never ending flow of people came to the celebration. They welcomed Billy Bob to the tribe, and then would leave after an hour or so. Almost every person brought a gift of some kind and presented it to Black Horse.

While I was standing next to Black Horse, a tall man dressed in typical old-style Comanche clothing walked up. Black Horse introduced him as the Chief or Head of the Council. It was Quanah Iron Coat himself. I had seen pictures of Quanah Parker and he closely resembled his great-great-grandfather. His bright eyes were the feature I noticed first.

Quanah Iron Coat was a handsome man and his long braided hair was also graying. You could tell he spent a lot of time outside because his facial skin was deeply tanned with crow's feet wrinkles around his eyes. He seemed like a kind caring person as he softly spoke to Black Horse. I didn't understand a word they were saying so I just listened to the wonderful Comanche language being spoken. It sounded almost like music.

I heard Black Horse switch in mid-sentence to English and mention my name. Quanah stepped up in front of me and shook my hand. "So, you are the one to bring Black Horse his son."

I was speechless meeting a great-grandson of Quanah Parker. "Yes, I brought him here, but at the time I didn't know who he was. It's really the work of God or just plain luck."

Nodding his head he folded his arms and looked at me. "So, you take no credit for finding Little Black Horse."

"No, not really. I mean yeah, I brought him

here, but I didn't plan it."

"Whether it was fate, luck, God, or the Great Spirit that brought him here, it does not matter. It is important that he is here now. My friend's heart is healed. You made that possible."

"I didn't do anything, but let Billy ride along with me."

"I like you Jack Gunn. You are an honest white man," Quanah Iron Coat said.

I didn't respond to Quanah because I couldn't think of anything to say at the time. After a minute, Black Horse said, "Quanah, Jack needs your help. He would like to look at the relics of metal Helmets and swords."

"Yes, he may see them, but they are not for sale."

I replied, "I just wanna look at them. I want to see if any have a Templar Cross on them."

"I don't know what a Templar Cross is, but you are welcome to my home to look at them."

"Can we see them now?"

Quanah laughed and replied, "No, not now. It is a night to celebrate the good news for my brother. Come in the morning and I will show you everything."

"How does 8 am sound?"

"That is ok." Without saying another word Quanah Iron Coat walked away, disappearing into the crowd of people.

I turned to observe Black Horse and his son

who were now mingling around in the crowd of people. I watched them as Black Horse proudly showed off his son.

I left the party and went to check on my men, most of whom were sitting around a campfire. Baldwin called me over. "I see you got a bunch of happy campers over there."

"Yeah, I'm happy for Billy Bob and Black Horse. It's funny how things work out."

"I take it you didn't find anything indicating that the Templars have been here?"

"No, not yet. Tomorrow the great-grandson of Quanah Parker is gonna show me his collection of metal helmets and stuff. Keep your fingers crossed."

I walked away and went to the motel room because it was already 11 pm. I needed a shot of JD, which was in the room. Opening the motel room door, I found Maggie and Adam there watching an old cowboy and indian movie, named The Searchers. Adolf and Freda were lying on the floor and sat up to greet me.

Maggie glanced up at me. "Well, what did you find?"

"Nothing, so far. Tomorrow Chief Quanah Iron Coat is gonna show me his pile of relics. Maybe I'll find something at his place."

Adam asked, "Can I come along?"

Before I could reply, Maggie said, "I wanna come along."

I poured a shot of JD and took a sip before

answering them. "Alright, you guys can come along. I don't think Quanah will mind."

I strolled outside for a smoke, and another drink. After that I went to bed. I couldn't fall asleep thinking about the possibility of finding something that proves the Templars visited here long ago.

WHITE GHOSTS
APRIL 27, 2026

The rooster woke me up again at 4 am. I wanted to shoot that damn thing. After a cup of Indian coffee with Big Buffalo and some food, we went to Quanah Iron Coat's house. Adam had hold of the dogs when Quanah opened the door. He was surprised by the dogs. He stepped outside to greet us.

"I forgot you were coming. What's your name again?"

"Jack Gunn, a friend of Black Horse."

He laughed a little. "Yes, that's right. You found Little Black Horse."

Iron Coat's house was a small dwelling which had a two car garage next to it. It was just a normal one-story ranch that was badly in need of a paint job, and possibly a new roof.

I introduced him to Adam and Maggie.

Looking at the dogs he asked, "What are the names of these wolf dogs?"

Pointing to each one Adam replied, "Adolf and Freda."

He bent down and the dogs smelled his hand. They let Quanah pet them. Their tails were wagging so I could tell they liked him. That put me at ease. Like I always say, dogs can sense if someone is of good character.

"Tie the wolf dogs up out here and come inside," Quanah said.

Stepping inside I could smell the mold or mildew. It was a musty odor that made me sneeze.

Quanah said, "Welcome to my home. I live alone since my wife passed away years ago. My three sons live 20 miles away, out in the country. I don't get many visitors.

The three of us just stood there viewing the piles of stuff, waiting for his approval to proceed with our search. "Go ahead and look around. There is junk all over the place because I never throw anything away."

I glanced around the room and there was stuff piled in every corner, knee deep. I pulled out a picture of the Templar Cross and showed it to him. "Have you ever seen this symbol on anything?"

He carefully looked at the picture. "Yes, I have seen that symbol, but I don't remember where. Let me think about it."

I thought; *does he have memory problems?*

It was clear that Quanah was a hoarder. His home was filled with all kinds of items, which he cherished. I told Maggie and Adam, "Ok, start looking around for anything that could have a Templar Cross on it, like a helmet, sword, or shield."

Mr. Quanah commented, "I know somewhere … somewhere … I have seen that symbol. Oh, there is also stuff in the garage."

I went to the garage to search. After two hours, my back and hands were killing me. I was only halfway done with the pile of relics and I was beat. I walked back into the living room to take a break.

I heard Maggie ask Quanah if he could turn on the light. He reached over from his chair to pull the chain on a lamp next to him. I watched him pull the chain and the lamp lit up, but it was far from being a bright light.

I asked, "Maggie, any luck?"

"No luck here, but I found a dead rat."

Quanah chuckled and said, "You may keep the rat."

Adam shouted from a back room. "No luck here."

I looked at Quanah and again at the lamp. I did a double take. The lamp had tassels hanging from it. I couldn't actually make out what it was until I moved closer to it. It was a homemade lamp alright. There was something underneath the lamp shade.

I took the shade off. Yes, underneath was a helmet. I carefully rubbed the dust off the helmet. To my surprise there was the Templar Cross etched into the side of it. I shouted, "This is it! Here's a Templars helmet!" Adam and Maggie stepped over the junk on the floor to view it.

Quanah said, "Yes, that's it. Now I remember. Let me see that." Removing the metal helmet from the lampstand, I handed the heavy thing to him. "I made this lamp from the helmet years ago, so I wouldn't lose it. This is very important. Let me tell you the story about this helmet."

"You have a story?" Adam asked.

"Yes, Black Horse is not the only one who knows stories. It is my family story from many thousands of moons ago. It is the story of how the Comanche tribe obtained the first horses from the White Ghosts."

"White Ghosts?"

"Yes, White Ghosts, Wolf Boy," Iron Coat said, with a laugh. "That is my Indian name for you. You are now Wolf Boy because of your wolf dogs."

Adam smiled and said, "Thank you for the Indian name, Mr. Quanah."

"Now, let me tell the story. It is a long story so sit down and listen carefully, because I will not repeat it." We quickly sat down as close as possible so we wouldn't miss a word from the soft spoken old man.

Quanah continued, "Hundreds of years ago, my people were living here on the plains. They had no horses at the time because the horse was not here then. They hunted on foot. They even hunted buffalo on foot which was dangerous and almost impossible.

"Only the fastest runners and best hunters could kill a buffalo using spears and arrows. It became a test of manhood. To become a man, you needed to kill a buffalo by yourself. A good hunter could do this by the age of fourteen."

Adam interrupted, "I'm almost fourteen. I can't imagine killing a buffalo with arrows, on foot. I think it's impossible."

"They had to do it or the tribe would go hungry. They would sneak up on the buffalo dressed as another buffalo. The hunter would need to get within 20 yards. Usually a group of men would go after one buffalo. It would take many arrows to kill a buffalo. Once it was shot, the buffalo would run so the hunters would have to run after it, until it stopped. Then they would shoot it again. When the buffalo dropped to the ground, then all would run in and stab it in the heart with spears."

Quanah asked for a glass of water which Adam swiftly brought him. "Ok, here's your water Mr. Quanah. Please, tell us more."

"After killing the buffalo, the hunters would cut out the liver and each would take a bite while it was still warm. They hold it in the air thanking the Buffalo Spirit for its life."

The old Indian stopped talking for a minute. As if he was trying to think what to say. "Oh, the women in the tribe cut the buffalo up and dragged it back to camp. Sometimes that would take all day depending how many miles they had to walk."

Maggie said, "Wow, that's a lot of work. One of those buffalo could weight a ton."

"One day the hunters were tracking a buffalo herd when they saw the White Ghosts. The ghosts were riding on the back of some strange animal. Of course, the hunters were surprised and frightened by what they saw. They wondered are these men, spirits, or ghosts? All were dressed in long white robes, their heads and faces were covered by masks, which we call metal helmets. The hunters had never seen anything like this before.

"They decided to follow these ghosts, to see what they were doing and where they were going. According to the story, there were more ghosts than they could count. They also had wagons which were pulled by the big animals. Remember, the Comanche nor any Indians ever used wagons. Indians didn't have the wheel a long time ago. Everything was moved by pulling a pole sled."

Quanah stopped talking and lit up a smoke. I stood up, stretched my legs, and also lit one up.

After a few puffs, he continued the story. "So our hunters wanted to watch these ghosts, which they did while keeping out of sight. They followed them for three days and nights. After that it was clear that they were not ghosts, but some type of man with white skin. They observed how the men took care of the big animals that they rode on. The hunters noticed that the animals ate grass like the buffalo.

"One the fourth day, the white men stopped to carve some stones. The hunters were spotted by the white robes. One of the white robes waved a hand at them to come into their camp. A group of white men rode to meet the hunters, who now were afraid. When the white men came to close, one hunter shot an arrow at him, out of fear. The arrow just bounced off the white man. The hunters thought he was arrow proof."

"The arrow bounced off because of the Knights armor," Adam said.

"The white men on their big animals surrounded the hunters and pointed their long knives at them."

Adam interjected, "You mean their swords."

Quanah gave Adam a look telling him to be quiet. "Yes, swords. When they took out the swords, the small group of hunters submitted, throwing down their weapons. They walked back to the camp of the white men under guard and were given some water."

"Wow," Adam responded.

"They tried to speak to each other but it was impossible. The hunters just sat there and watched the white robes carve a rock for five days."

Old Quanah stopped talking and looked at the helmet. As he rubbed the helmet it seemed his mind was racing back in time. Back to a time of the Comanche hunters, so long ago. I'm sure every time he told this story he held the helmet in his hands. It probably helped him to remember.

After a long pause, Adam asked, “So what did they do?”

“The white eyes fell asleep during the night. The hunters killed two of them and snuck away without being heard.”

“That’s it?” Adam asked. “What about the horses?”

“Oh yes, I forgot. They took four horses with them and this helmet. That is the story how the Comanche was the first tribe to have the horse.”

“Didn’t the Knights chase them?” Maggie asked.

“I do not know if they did,” Quanah replied. “That is the end of the story. I don’t remember any more right now.”

I asked, “What about the rock they were carving?”

“Oh, it is still there on a hill, near the old trail.”

I stood up and thought, *if the carved rock is still there it may have the Templar Cross carved in it or some clue.* “Mr. Quanah, can you take us to this carved rock?”

“Sure, but it is just a rock. It has the same symbol as the helmet on it.”

“You said the rock is near the old trail. Can you tell us how to go there?”

“Maybe I can remember where it is. Why do you want to see a rock?”

Maggie touched the old Chief’s hand and

softly said, "Mr. Quanah, the rock, and trail are important for us to see. Will you please take us to see it?"

"Yes, I would like to, but I'm too old for that. It is a two day journey by pony. I have no ponies."

I laughed a little and said, "We'll go by truck."

"I have no truck."

"Chief Quanah, we have a truck."

Maggie spoke up. "Mr. Quanah, we have a truck so you can ride in comfort, so please show us the rock."

He looked at Maggie and patted her head. "Ok, Warrior Woman, who carries a long knife. I will take you. Make ready to leave."

Quanah was referring to the fact that Maggie was dressed in combat fatigues, carried an M4, and had her machete dangling from her waist. She was an imposing figure, so to speak. It was hard to say no to Maggie when she asked you a soft sweet voice for a favor.

We made the truck ready and advised Captain Baldwin where we were going. The only problem was we didn't know exactly where we were going. The Chief just told us he'd remember as he went along.

Pulling away from Lawton we headed north on Route 281 per the Chief's directions. It was almost 2 pm. It was a cloudy day and you could sense that some rainstorms were heading our way.

After about an hour, Iron Coat said, "Slow down and turn left here." I slowed down and started to turn. "No, don't turn here, keep going a little more."

I had my doubts that he could remember where the trail was. At the next dirt road, Quanah told me to turn left. "Is this the correct trail?" I asked, as I stopped the truck.

"Yes, it is. Keep going straight on this road until I tell you to stop."

This wasn't a road at all. It was a single lane dirt trail with big ruts in it. The terrain next to the trail was rocky and contained little valleys or dips. In my opinion, the terrain was impassable, even by four-wheel drive.

We had to slow down to keep from breaking an axle or getting a flat tire on the sharp rocks. The whole truck was rocking and rolling, making everyone hold on to something to keep stable. Our speed was a blazing 5 to 10 mph.

Chief Quanah dozed off and his head was shaking like a bobblehead doll. That disturbed me because if he was asleep, we could drive right past the Templar location and not know it.

The shaking, rocking, and rolling of the truck was getting to everyone. Maggie said, "Man this is a rough road. I'm getting sea sick."

Adam laughed. "It's fun, Maggie."

I said, "Look out the window at the horizon. Don't look at the floor or you'll get sick."

Quanah woke up in a daze. Adam asked, "Mr. Quanah, how much further?"

"I don't know. This looks different from the old days."

I said, "We're stopping here for a break." I figured that we needed a break, and maybe if Quanah got out of the truck, and looked around it might spark his memory. Maybe riding in the truck was confusing him, since he was probably here last on horseback.

I pulled to a stop on top of a small knoll. We all got out and stretched our legs. The dogs gladly jumped out and started running around. I gave the Chief a smoke, and we both lit up. Maggie handed us all a bottle of water. As I walked around the dirt trail, I couldn't help but think that this was the old Army trail, which was originally an Indian trail. This had been here hundreds of years. If the Knights Templar used this trail, I couldn't imagine how they ever pulled wagons over this. It must have been slow going.

I walked over to Quanah who was sitting on a big stone. "Chief, how do you feel?"

"Better since we stopped. I was getting sick also. A pony is better on this trail."

"I agree a pony is better. Do you know how much further?"

He peered down the trail and pointed. "You see that high hill? The one far away, with the flat top."

"Yes, I see it."

"I think that is Ghost Hill. We'll know if it is, when we get there"

Looking at the hill through my M4 scope, I

estimated the hill was a couple of hours away at the speed we were going.

Mounting up we got moving again. Dark clouds rolled in and it started to rain. If it rained a lot this dirt trail could turn into a mud slick path, making it dangerous as hell. There were cliffs on both sides of the road which meant possible death, if we slid off.

I stopped at the bottom of the big hill and observed the trail had a 30 degree incline. It started pouring cats and dogs. Water was running down the dirt trail like rain in a gutter. The road was being flooded. I dropped the transmission into 4- wheel drive low. Thank God, for big knobby off-road tires.

I muttered, "Everyone hold on, here we go."

My trusty F-250 slowly groaned forward in low gear. The wheels were spinning every now and then. The trail being only seven to eight feet wide didn't leave much room for error. All of a sudden I lost traction and the rear end skidded off to the side.

Maggie shouted, "Oh my, God!"

I stopped as Maggie looked out the rear window. "Jack, this left rear tire is almost hanging over the cliff."

I counter steered just a little while slowly applying gas to inch forward, trying not to spin the wheels. It worked and we inched forward making it to the top of the hill. Of course, as soon as we got on top the driving rain changed to a slight drizzle.

Chief Quanah said, "It is the rainy season." We all laughed at that comment because he seemed unconcerned about the dangerous situation we just had.

Coming to a stop I said, "I need a drink." Getting out of the truck, I lit up a smoke.

Maggie handed me my bottle of JD. I took two big swigs and handed it back to her. She asked, "Is this it?"

"Yes, welcome to Ghost Hill," Quanah said.

The top of the hill was flat, and was the size of a football field. It was made up of huge rocks protruding out of the ground. These rocks, some the size of cars, were lying all over the top of the hill. There must have been thirty of them.

The Chief was still sitting in the truck. I asked, "Do you know which rock is carved?"

"I can't remember which one."

I ordered, "Maggie, Adam, let's spread out and check each stone."

It was getting dark early, due to the rain clouds. As I walked around checking each rock, I knew we couldn't go back to Lawton tonight with the rain and mud. It was simply too dangerous. I visualized us sliding down the muddy hill, out of control, and going over the cliff.

Adam yelled, "I found one!" Maggie and I ran over to see it. Carved in the top was an arrow. I checked my compass and it pointed due west.

Further to the north, I spotted a gravestone shaped like a Templar Cross. Just the top of it was protruding from the ground. We walked over to it and found another one that was almost completely buried. I said, "Two grave markers means two dead men; just like the Chief told us in his story."

It was a little spooky finding the graves. No one spoke a word because it was almost like we were standing on holy ground.

Maggie checked another big stone near it and found another Templar Cross engraved in the rock. We stood there observing this stone. Adam and I ran our hands over the worn stone. These stones were confirmation that the Knights were here long before any other Europeans. This validated that we were on the right track to find the treasure.

Adam took some pictures of the stones. While standing on top of the rock, he pointed towards the trail. "Look, there's some trucks coming."

I quickly turned around to observe them. I counted eight trucks about a mile away. I ran to get my Cobb 50 out of our truck, because the scope would give me a better view.

Using the high power scope, I could see someone's face, up to almost a mile away. Placing the big rifle's bipod on a stone, I peered through the scope. The first vehicle was the black truck that had been dogging us since Florida.

I used the zoom to gain a closer view. The trucks stopped about 800 yards away, according to my laser range finder. Watching them dismount, the man driving the black truck got out and looked directly at the hill. All of the men had on the Templar white surcoats, with the red cross on the front. I called Adam over. "Adam, here take a look. Who is this guy?"

Adam peered into the scope and replied, "I can't believe it. I think it's Mr. Canfield. It's hard to tell because he's got a hat on."

"I thought that was him. The rat is after you and the Sword of Jerusalem."

Canfield is the man who tried to stop Adam and Emma from coming to live with me the night Adam's grandfather passed away. He is a corrupted member of the old order of the Knights Templar. He and Christian de Molay had planned to steal the Sword of Jerusalem in order to find the treasure.

Chief Quanah walked over and asked, "What is going on?" He peered down the hill and saw the white mantles. "We have brought the White Ghosts back to life. It was not good to come here."

"Quanah, they aren't Ghosts. They're men just like us. Watch, I'll show you." I moved Adam aside. I bent down on one knee, and squinted through the scope at my target. I wanted to take this guy out. I wanted this asshole dead.

"If they are men, like us, why do they come here dressed like ghosts?"

"It's a long story why they're here. I'll tell you later, Chief."

These were dangerous men who wanted the sword and the treasure for their own profit. I had no choice but to try and kill their leader, Mr. Canfield, and maybe a few others. If I could terminate a couple, from this distance, maybe they would think twice before coming any closer.

Racking a round into the chamber, I looked through the scope. Canfield's head came into view. I zeroed the cross hairs on his chest. Quickly, I checked the bushes for wind. There was about a 15 mph breeze from the south. I adjusted my scope to compensate for windage, by 3 clicks. I knew this Cobb was zeroed in for 1,000 yards. The 200 yard difference wouldn't matter much, since I was shooting downhill. I decided to aim at his center of mass. It didn't matter much where I hit him, because the 50 caliber round would blow him apart. This was a long shot, almost a half mile, and even a raindrop could cause me to miss.

Iron Coat asked, "Are you going to kill them?"

"Yes, they're here to steal the sword and possibly kidnap Adam. Everyone hold your ears."

"If you can kill the ghosts, I will name you, Ghost Killer."

Canfield was pointing at us on top the hill. I doubted he could see us and saw only our truck. Then he pulled out binoculars and gazed at the hill. Observing him while he was scanning the hill was chilling, to say the least. Little did he realize a bullet would soon rip into him.

Then he looked directly at us. I told Adam to wave at him. Canfield did a double take and then the fool waved back. While he looked at us, I squeezed the trigger. KABOOM, the rifle recoiled, and I pulled back on target for another shot.

I didn't need it because my round flew straight and true, hitting the target, cutting him almost in half. His white robe turned blood red. The rest of his men ducked for cover. I spotted another man sticking his head up on the other side of the black truck, from behind a door. I fired again, KABOOM. The superman bullet went through the door and killed him. The other trucks started to quickly back-up trying to get out of range.

I let them go for now, knowing that come morning we may have to fight our way out of this mess. I had to come up with a plan tonight.

Quanah said, "I have never seen a white man kill another white man."

"Believe me Chief, I've killed many bad white men over the years."

"I believe you, Ghost Killer."

It was going to be a long night. I posted Adam, with my M4, to watch the dirt trail on the east side. Maggie was assigned to the west side of the hill along with Freda.

The Chief was sitting in the truck so he could watch the south. I wasn't worried about the south because it had a 30 foot drop off. I gave him my

Glock 17 to use just in case. He smiled at me when I handed him the gun and told him, "If you see any ghosts shoot them." He laughed a little and nodded.

I covered the north side of the hill with Adolf by my side. If they were going to attack us this was the most likely direction they would come from, because the terrain was almost flat.

I wondered, how in the hell did these guys find us. The only thing I could think of was there had to be a GPS bug hidden somewhere. Then it hit me. The most likely place would be in the sword case.

Sitting there, I thought about using my satellite phone to call Baldwin. Maybe he could get a GPS fix on our location and come to our rescue. I turned it on, but with the thick cloud cover I couldn't receive a signal. It was dark now, and the clouds blocked out the moon. A fog was starting to descend on us.

I hunkered down, next to a big stone, with Adolf. He glanced at me, so I rubbed his damp head, and said, "I need to make a plan. Adolf, you got any ideas?"

If they attacked us I guessed it would be early in the morning, about 4am.

It was sometime after midnight and the fog, which now covered the top of Ghost Hill, created a light cold mist. As it slowly moved down the hill, visibility was reduced to a hundred feet, making it almost impossible to see a damn thing.

I told Adolf, "Sit, guard." Giving him that

order, he would not fall asleep; he would sit there all night on full alert. Those command words made him raise his ears and visually scan the area. His nose was sniffing the air for the scent of any human.

Adolf, my German Sheppard guard dog, doesn't miss a thing. With him by my side I knew no one could come within fifty yards of me. I sat down next to him and pulled my collar up to keep the wet chilly mist from going down my neck.

My friend Rick and I rescued Adolf and three other dogs from a kennel, not far from Tocabaga. The trainer and owner, an old German man named Klaus, was murdered by someone and the dogs were running loose. It was just plain luck that we went to his house to purchase a couple of trained guard dogs and found him. Klaus had been a friend of Rick's for five years. Anyway, we saved the dogs and they became valuable allies for us. By the way, we also found the body of a man that the dogs had apparently killed. We assumed it was the same person who murdered Mr. Klaus, because there was a gun in his dead hand.

Pulling a pack of smokes out of my vest pocket, I noted there were only three left. I lit one up to take off the edge, took a few drags, and then snuffed it out with my fingers to save the butt for later. If I ran out of smokes it would piss me off. I know smoking is bad for you, but when your number is up, it's up. That's the way I look at it. No one can live forever.

I'm not worried about dying because we all die, and I believe there is life after death. I guess that's why I'm not afraid to get into gun fights. I never think about getting killed because if you do, then you will get killed.

There were about fifteen men in the convoy of cars down the trail. Fifteen men against four, doesn't give us very good odds. Our options were: sit here, wait for an attack, and build a defensive line of some kind. Leave the hill tonight, head west on the old trail, and try to out run them, or scout them out and attack them first. We could snipe them off one by one.

Pondering our options, I thought, leaving the hill tonight was just asking for trouble on the mud-slick narrow trail. We could wind-up sliding off the road into a ditch. Then we'd be stuck in the middle of nowhere.

The smartest thing to do is to build some type of defensive line. Picking them off one by one could be the best choice. Yes, it's dangerous but it could put enough fear into them to leave. They had no idea how many men we have on top the hill.

I decided to use two of the options. We'll make a defensive line and snipe off as many as possible. I rubbed Adolf's head. It was soaking wet. He looked at me to give him a command. I said, "Good boy. Sit, guard." He didn't seem to mind a little rain. Every now and then he'd get up and shake off the water.

To snipe these guys without getting caught, I would need a silencer. I had one for my M4, so I needed to get my gun from Adam. That, however, would leave him without a weapon. It occurred to me that Maggie had a pistol with her, so I'd have to run over and obtain it for Adam.

I looked at Adolf and pointed my finger at him. "Sit, guard, stay." Adolf understood my command and didn't follow me as I jogged over to Maggie's position.

I couldn't even see her in the foggy mist. She was well hidden. I shouted in a loud whisper, "Maggie, it's Jack."

After a few calls, she peeked her head out from behind a rock. "Over here," Maggie replied, in a soft tone.

I scooted behind the big rock, sitting down next to her. "How you doing?"

"Ok, just cold and wet."

I explained my plan to her. She said, "I got a better plan."

Surprised, I said, "Ok, tell me."

"We'll leave the two dogs with Adam. He knows how to control them. Adam and the Chief can guard the truck; we'll leave them our pistols. You and I sneak down the hill and kill these guys."

I thought about it for a minute. "Ok, I agree. My guess is these guys are just sitting in their cars waiting for daylight, trying to stay warm and dry. Meet me at the truck. I have to get Adolf."

I figured that two of us going would be better than just one. We could cover each other and it would double our fire power if we got into a fire fight.

Meeting Maggie at the truck, we informed Adam of our plan. He was a little concerned about us leaving him and Quanah alone. I was also a little worried about leaving a thirteen-year-old kid to guard old Mr. Quanah. But, I knew the old Templars were not really after us. They wanted the Sword of Jerusalem and possibly Adam, because he could read the Latin writing.

I unscrewed the flash suppressors on the M4s and put on the silencers. We would have to make head shots to drop our targets quickly before they could fire a round or yell out a warning. Like all snipers say, 'one shot, one kill.' If we could kill five or six of them I'd be a happy camper, or should I say a happy sniper.

Leaving both dogs with Adam, I advised him to use the big rock near the truck for cover. If he saw anyone, then order the dogs to attack. If they get by the dogs, then shoot as many as you can. He had Maggie's Glock, and we gave him twenty magazines.

I woke up Quanah. "Chief, we need your help."

He rubbed his eyes and replied, "What do you need?"

"I need you to stand guard with Adam while Maggie and I go on a scouting mission."

"You are going to leave us here?"

"Yes, for a short time. The wolf dogs will stay with you."

Adam spoke up, "Don't worry, Mr. Quanah, I'm a good shot."

Quanah Iron Coat laughed and said, "That is good, Wolf Boy. Ghost Killer, how long will you be gone?"

As Maggie and I checked our gear, I said, "Maybe two hours. If we hear any gunfire we'll scamper back here fast." I could tell that Quanah was uneasy about us leaving him alone with Adam for protection. He didn't know that Adam was a trained deadly shot. I spent the last six months training him four hours per day the necessary combat shooting skills.

Maggie and I had on our normal black SWAT-like combat gear. Our BPV's could stop an AK round. The M4s have FLIR night vision scopes which allow us to see the body heat of our enemies in the fog and darkness. The main problem is these scopes greatly reduce the distance you can clearly see due to a lack of resolution at over 200 yards. We'd have to be within 50 yards to make a good head shot.

The one item we didn't have with us was our tactical radio gear, which would permit us to communicate quietly over a distance. This meant we would have to maintain visual contact with each other. I suggested we keep no more than twenty to thirty feet apart. I would take the point and Maggie would protect our backsides.

We slowly walked to the north side to make our way down the hill. My plan was to flank them from the north. At the bottom of the hill, the terrain was rocky but mostly flat, covered with small trees, bushes, and knee high prairie grass.

Before proceeding down the hill, we knelt down and scanned the entire area with our night vision for about 10 minutes. I saw a couple of animals, one in a tree, and another on the ground. It looked scary peering into the fog not knowing what the hell was out there.

Satisfied that the bottom of the hill was clear, we slid down the steep wet slope and stopped to scan around again. Maggie and I mudded up our faces, so no white skin was showing. Standing there waiting for Maggie, I took a deep breath and a voice in my head said, *'Go ahead. There is nothing to be afraid of.'*

I calculated we would have to travel east about one klick or 1000 meters, which is 0.62 miles. I would pace that off counting my steps. It's common practice to use 110 paces to equal 100 meters on flat ground. When we reach 1,100 paces we would turn south, towards the old trail where the enemy was located.

Proceeding forward, I checked the compass to make sure we were heading due east. We were moving east, parallel to the trail, and were probably a quarter mile north of it. Maggie was thirty feet behind me. I estimated we could only see about fifty to a hundred feet in front of us because of the thick dense fog. It was slow going because I halted every 10 paces to look and listen for a minute. I kept count of my paces so we wouldn't get lost in the fog.

Finally, after almost an hour of walking, I heard voices. I raised my hand signaling Maggie to stop, and waved her up to me.

We heard one man say, "You guys finish turning around the trucks so we can get out of here. I gotta take a leak."

Peering through our scopes we spotted him walking towards us. Ducking down into the thick mist and high grass, behind a bush, we watched him approach. He stopped right on the other side of the bush we were hiding behind. He was so close we could hear the sound of his urine splashing the ground.

As soon as he was finished, he turned around to walk back to his men. I silently stood up, took aim through my scope, and fired one round into the back of his head. He dropped dead as a doornail. Grabbing him by his feet, I dragged him back into the high grass, about 40 feet away, while Maggie kept a look-out.

Another man yelled, "Hey Marco! Hurry up."

Since Marco couldn't reply, I knew someone would come looking for him.

Maggie and I made ready to pop the next jerk. We spread out, about 50 feet apart. Whoever was closest to bogey would take him out.

He yelled again, but his voice was closer this

time. "Marco, what the hell are you doing?"

As he came into view, Maggie had the shot. He was less than thirty feet from Maggie when she popped him. His body stood still, but he didn't fall. Maggie fired again popping him in the melon and so did I. He dropped like a box full of rocks.

We moved forward to obtain a view of the trucks. All the men were inside the vehicles, and the headlights were on. Maggie was on my right flank as we laid in the high grass about fifty feet away from the targets. I whispered, "If anyone else gets out of the trucks shoot them."

Sure enough, a third man climbed out of the last truck, and started shouting for the two we had just killed. I gave the signal to fire. We both started firing short bursts on full auto and he fell dead next to the truck. Another person yelled, "Someone's shooting at us! They just killed Eddy. Let's get the hell out of here!" We kept peppering the trucks with short bursts hoping to kill a few more.

"What about Marco and Greg," another shouted, as they fired wild shots into the foggy night, some of which zipped over our heads. They had no idea we were so close to them.

The last thing I heard was, "We can't help them. Let's get the hell out of here before we get killed!"

They started to pull away and we ceased fire. They didn't have the stomach for a gun battle. As we watched the trucks quickly pull away I thought, *how lucky we were. Or was it luck?*

Maggie and I stood on the trail watching their taillights fade away into the fog and darkness. We turned around without saying a word to each other and started back up Ghost Hill.

Halfway up, Maggie said, "Mission accomplished. I need a shot of JD when we get back."

Out of breath I said, "Me … too."

"I'm glad they're gone."

"Yeah it was almost too easy. We haven't seen the last of them," I replied. "I'm sure … we'll see a couple of their trucks … in the ravine, on our way back."

We slowly trudged back up the steep hill. Near the top, I shouted, "Adam, we're coming in! Don't shoot!"

Adam and the dogs ran over to greet us. "You guys ok?" he asked.

"Yeah, they left when we started shooting them."

Quanah asked, "Did you kill more Ghosts?"

Maggie replied, "Yeah, but it was no big deal, Chief."

I said, "I gotta eat something to get my energy back."

Maggie broke out the portable stove and started to heat some MREs up for everyone. We had gone all day and night with no grub. While she was cooking, we each had a couple shots of JD.

Maggie handed an MRE to the Chief. He smelled it and asked, "What is this?"

Adam said, "It's Army food."

"It smells like dog food."

"Hold your nose and eat it. It's good for you," Maggie told him. "See the dogs like it." Both dogs had gobbled down the MREs before we even had taken a bite.

Changing the subject, I said, "Ok, here's the plan. We'll eat and rest here until the sun comes out and dries up the trail a little. I wanna leave by noon."

POWER OF THE SWORD
APRIL 28, 2026

The sun was just starting to rise and the sky was clearing up. It looked like it was going to be a nice day.

We cleaned our weapons and were in the process of getting ready to move out, when Maggie spotted some vehicles heading our way. I looked at them using the Cobb 50 scope. To my surprise, it was two of our Humvees coming to the rescue.

Half an hour later, Captain Baldwin, Black Horse, and Walker climbed out of the first truck. I greeted them all with a hand shake. "Boy, I'm glad to see you guys. How did you find us?"

Baldwin said, "Oh, we have our ways. When you didn't come back yesterday, I figured something must have happened."

"Did you see any other trucks on your way

here?"

"No, why?"

"Well, we had a little run in with the old Templars last night."

"What happened?"

"I killed Canfield and another guy. Then Maggie and I sniped them, killing three more. Then they left. End of story. Maybe with Canfield dead, they'll stop chasing us for the sword."

Baldwin shrugged his shoulders. "Maybe they will, maybe they won't. We have to find out how they're tracking us."

"Thanks for reminding me. Adam, bring me the sword. I wanna check the box for a GPS bug."

Adam said, "Ok, but there's no bug in it. I know every little thing about that box." Adam got up and went to remove the box from under the back seat of the truck.

He came running over to me. "Something is wrong." He placed the sword box on a rock and opened it. We looked inside and were shocked to see a wooden branch along with a note written in Latin.

Adam read it out loud. "The treasure belongs to those who find it."

"They got the sword and this note means they can read Latin," I exclaimed, while looking at Adam. "How in the hell did this happen?"

"I don't know, Grandpa."

Quanah said, "I know, maybe a ghost took it."

I inquired, "Did you see anyone, Chief?"

"I saw no one."

"Where were you at, Adam?" I asked.

Adam hung his head down. "It must have happened when we took the dogs for a little walk around the hill top."

"Shit, these guys sneak right into our camp and steal the most important item we have." I was upset because I thought Adam would know better than to leave the sword unguarded. On the other hand, it was also my fault for leaving Adam and Quanah alone.

I carefully felt around inside the silk-lined wooden box. Running my fingers over the cloth, on all sides, and feeling the corners. In one corner, I felt a bump the size of a quarter. "I think the bug is here."

Pulling out my knife I made a slit just big enough to remove the item. Adam said, "Please be careful, don't damage the box."

Using my fingers, I lifted it out. It was a GPS bug alright, about the size of a quarter, but a little thicker. I held it up for everyone to see. Then I smashed it into pieces with a stone.

Maggie said, "They must have been watching us. When no one was around, they came to the truck and took the sword."

Baldwin butted in, "Don't worry we'll get that sword back. How long ago did they leave?"

"It was around 4 am," I said.

"Which way do you think they'll go, Jack?"

"If I was them, I'd go back to Route 281, then go to I-40 and head west. They certainly can't go to Lawton. One thing to our advantage is they still have to figure out what the clues mean."

Adam said, "Yeah, that could take them weeks."

"They'll need to stop somewhere and study the sword clues."

Baldwin said, "We can't go back the way we came because our trucks are too slow. We'll never catch them once they're on I-40. Does anyone know where this trail goes to?"

Black Horse replied, "It goes all the way to Amarillo. Up ahead, about 10 miles, it runs into Route 183. We can get on 183 and then it is just a few miles to I-40. There is an intersection there."

"Good, maybe we can cut them off and ambush them at the intersection. Everyone mount up. Let's roll."

Pulling off of Ghost Hill, heading west, the Hummers took the lead. They could make faster time than my F-250 on the bumpy trail. It wasn't long before they were out of sight.

On the way, Adam commented, "If they unsheathe the sword and touch the blade, God will punish them if they're not worthy."

Maggie asked, "What do you mean?"

"I'm just saying something bad could happen. That's why I told Grandpa Jack not to touch the sword blade."

"Oh, I'm not worthy in the eyes of God," I commented.

"Maybe you are and maybe you're not, but that is up to God. I just didn't want anything bad to happen to you."

After seeing with my own eyes, the sword behead Christian de Molay in a flash of light, guided by the hand of an unseen Angel, I knew its power. Adam was right, don't touch the sword unless God tells you to. It sounds so crazy, I can hardly believe it myself.

"What if they are worthy?" Maggie asked.

"Then they will have the power of the sword," Adam said.

"What does that mean?" I asked.

Adam replied, "I don't really know what it means or what will happen. I only know they'll have the treasure map."

Chief Quanah asked, "What the hell are you talking about?"

"It's a long story, Chief, and we'll tell you later," I said. No one spoke after that. Adam's words gave us all a lot to think about. I thought, *maybe we should just let them have the sword.*

Driving along, it occurred to me, that Adam doesn't control the sword, it controls him. What if we find the treasure, then what will we do with it? Will God like the fact that we found his treasure? Will the power of the sword and possibly the Arc of the Covenant strike us down? Are the Bible stories about its power really true?

The more I thought about it, the more I wondered if we were doing the right thing. If God wanted us to find the treasure, why is he making it so darn difficult?

After an hour of a bumpy motion sickness on the old trail, we reached Route 183. I put the pedal to the metal to catch up to Captain Baldwin. He was already at the cloverleaf intersection preparing for the ambush.

We observed various cars and trucks zooming down the highway past our positions, headed west. I carefully peered at each one to make sure they weren't the old Templars.

A couple of hours had gone by, and the old Templar convoy still hadn't shown up. I tried to flag down a car, headed west, but it didn't wanna stop until we pointed our guns at the driver.

The driver, a young looking man who was clearly afraid of us, advised me that he saw some trucks back down the road, at a rest stop. In the car with him were four little kids, and I assumed the woman was his wife. He asked me if we could spare some food for his kids. Maggie gave them a box of MREs for helping us out. The woman thanked us and said, 'God Bless y'all,' and they drove away.

I couldn't help but wonder where this young man was going and why was he putting his family in danger. Driving on the expressway is dangerous because of Free Roamers, terrorists, and just plain terrible people who would kill you for your car and money, if you had any. His kids could be taken and sold as slaves to the highest bidder, or a sicko child molester could get them. They are the scum of the earth and I've killed a few of them over the years, I'm proud to say.

Everyone mounted up and we drove east to find the rest stop and possibly the Templar convoy. After twenty minutes, we spotted them and pulled over to check them out, from half a mile away. Pulling out the binoculars Baldwin and I carefully scanned the group of trucks. From the angle we were at, we couldn't see anyone moving around.

I commented, "They're checking out the sword and licking their wounds."

Baldwin said, "Here's the plan. We'll enter the rest stop from two sides, using the entrance and exit ramp, cutting them off so they can't escape. If they don't surrender and shoot at us, we'll blast them to hell. Jack, you follow my Humvee."

Everyone agreed with the plan so it was put into motion. We zoomed into the rest area as fast as possible, but saw no people. The Templars convoy was in a single line along the grassy area, next to some picnic tables. We could only see the driver's side of the vehicles and not the passenger side of their trucks.

It was strange that no one was visible. Baldwin yelled, "Be careful it could be a trap!"

Everyone dismounted with guns ready and surrounded the Templars pickup trucks. Adam and the Chief stayed in my truck as we started the search.

Rounding the front of the black pickup, I stopped dead in my tracks, as did the others in my group. On the ground lay the old Templars in their white mantles. They were clearly all dead.

It was a shocking sight as none of them had eyes and their faces were charred black. Lower jaws hung down, leaving mouths wide open, as if they were screaming. I could almost hear their cries of pain. It was abnormal because other parts of the bodies were untouched. The white mantels, which displayed the crimson cross, were not burned in any manner. There wasn't a drop of blood to be seen.

All twelve bodies looked identical, with burned out eyeballs and charred black faces. The old Templars were all laying on their backs, in a distorted twisted manner, with their hollow eye sockets facing the sky. It was an unearthly sight which told you supernatural forces were at work. The bodies were in a semi-circle around the Sword of Jerusalem, which was stuck straight into the ground about four inches deep. The scabbard was a few feet away, on the grass.

I glared at the blade, which was glowing red, pulsating on and off. The metal blade looked red hot, like it just came from a blacksmith's forge. I shouted, "Don't touch the sword! Don't go near it." All our men, including Baldwin, stopped dead in their tracks. Some of the warriors backed away a few more feet. "Adam, come over here right now!"

Adam came running and stopped next to me

when he saw the awful sight. He commented, "They touched the sword. God didn't deem them worthy and struck them down."

Adam started to move towards the sword, but I grabbed his arm, stopping him. "Do you think it's wise to touch the sword after seeing this?"

"I need to clean it and put it back in its scabbard. Once in the scabbard, everyone will be safe."

Still holding his arm, I asked, "Are you sure it won't hurt you?"

"Yes, I'm sure, Grandpa. Don't worry so much." I released is arm.

Adam walked up to the sword and it started flashing faster and faster. Adam slowly reached out to take hold of the handle. Suddenly, when his hand touched the grip, the sword turned glowing white, like a light bulb. It flashed the same intense white light as when the sword killed Christian de Molay.

Adam didn't move for a few seconds, it was as if he was frozen. I yelled, "Adam, are you ok?" He didn't reply. I moved closer to my grandson. I wasn't sure what action to take, if any. Was he being hurt by the sword? It sure appeared so to me. His body started to shake and his head was looking straight up at the sky.

Without further concern about myself, I grabbed his arm to pull him away and felt a force, almost like an electric shock. A strong tingling ran through my body. Frozen in place I couldn't remove my hand from Adam's arm. I tried with all my strength to pull my hand away, but I couldn't escape from the connection. I thought, *we're being electrocuted.*

Yet, it was a slightly different feeling. I can't explain it exactly, but it was a force or power that didn't actually hurt. The force was probing my body and brain. Yes, it was probing my brain. It was reading my memory. My life flashed before my eyes. It ran like a 3-D movie in my head. I saw everything I had done. All the good times and bad times of my life were on display. The people I had killed were in the movie. I clearly saw their faces as I killed them for a second time.

There was Leroy, the guy I killed with a shotgun, blowing off his head. Leroy was the scumbag doper who murdered my little brother, Mike, while he was in line at a burger place. Leroy killed little Mike in cold blood and only received a six year sentence. My brother Ron and I made a plan to kill his ass, when he got out of jail.

We ambushed him at a stoplight and I pulled the trigger from ten feet away, as he went for his gun. His head exploded like a ripe watermelon. It was an eye for an eye, because no one was going to murder my brother and get away with it. It was the first premeditated murder I had committed. But, I didn't think of it as murder. To me it was justice. 'Vengeance is Mine,' saith the Lord, and I was his instrument.

I was being judged for everything I ever did in

my life, whether it was good or bad. All these memories, some of which I didn't like, were popping up in the front of my head, zooming by incredibly fast.

I faintly heard Baldwin and Maggie yelling at me. Finally, I freed my hand from Adam, and I fell to the ground. Baldwin helped me up, just in time to see Adam pull the sword from the ground, point the blade at the sky, and kiss the ruby handle. The white glow suddenly stopped. He wiped off the blade, and slid it into the scabbard.

Adam asked, "Are you ok, Grandpa?"

"I … I think so. Are you alright?" I replied, still dazed by what just occurred.

"Yes, I'm fine. We were just judged to see if we were worthy to receive the sword."

"Has this happened to you before?"

"Yes, a couple of times."

"Baldwin, how long were we connected to the sword."

"Maybe ten or fifteen seconds, why?"

"Because, it seemed like hours. My whole life flashed in front of my eyes."

Adam laughed and said, "That's right, it was reading your life. Now I know why Grandpa De Molay chose you to be my guardian. He knew you would be worthy to handle the sword."

Maggie asked, "Adam, how does the sword do that? Is it controlled by God or an Angel?"

"I don't really know for sure. The sword

doesn't talk. I only know that God has spoken to me in my dreams."

Captain Baldwin said, "Glory to God." All his men repeated it in unison and made the sign of the cross.

Baldwin commented, "You see men, Adam does own the Power of the Holy Sword. This is the second time the sword has helped him."

Adam replied, "I'm only the caretaker of this sword, not the owner. No one can own God's treasure." After saying that, he put the sword in the box, and placed it under the backseat of my truck. I, for one, was glad that he did.

While watching the Templar Warriors dig graves, Chief Quanah and Black Horse were talking to Walker in Comanche. I had no idea what was being said, but I guessed they asked Walker how the sword could glow like it was on fire, and how did it kill all those men?

Baldwin and his men buried the old Templars in shallow graves. He said a prayer over each man, asking God to forgive them for their sins. After that we mounted up and headed back to the safety of the Comanche Nation.

Arriving there without further incidents, we parted ways with our Comanche friends for the night. When we dropped Chief Quanah off at his home, he commented, "Ghost Killer, you will have to tell the tribe stories of our trip. It was exciting for an old man. I need rest now."

We told the Chief good night. With no further comments, he turned and with shoulders slumped, walked slowly into his house.

Maggie asked, "Do you think he'll be alright?"

"Yeah, he's just tired like me," I said.

At the motel room, I pulled out my bottle of JD and had a few drinks to wind down. We were so worn out from the lack of sleep that we didn't bother to eat anything. Adam fell fast asleep on the floor with the dogs nuzzled up next to him. Maggie flopped into her bed still wearing her combat gear.

As I was dozing off, I couldn't help but wonder what the future had planned for us. I'll find out soon enough, like it or not.

Signing off for now.

GOD BLESS AMERICA, LAND OF THE FREE, and HOME OF THE BRAVE!

Jack Gunn, a.k.a. Tocabaga Jack

If you have any ideas where the treasure is located, let me know.

Email me at tocabaga.jack@gmail.com.

I WILL REPLY.

DRAMATIS PERSONAE TEMPLARS QUEST

Adam de Molay – A future Knights Templar leader. Sent to Jack Gunn, by God.
Black Horse – Medicine man for the Comanche Nation and father of Billy Bob.
Big Bear – An old Indian who runs the Comanche Nation Motel.
Billy Bob – Lost son of Black Horse who lived in Indianola Mississippi.
Canfield – A Templar of the old order, who wants to steal the Sword of Jerusalem.
Captain George Baldwin – A Knights Templar commander, of the new order.
Captain Sessions – Combat officer, commands and controls combat operations in the field.
Christian de Molay – Adam de Molay's uncle. A self proclaimed Grand Master.
Emma de Molay – The sister of Adam found on Interstate 75.
Jeff – Third in command of the new Templar order.
Grandpa Jack – Jack de Moley the Knights Templar Grand Master.
Hemmi – Wife of Jack Gunn.
Walker – James Walker, Captain of the Texas Rangers and nephew of Black Horse.
Jim Bo – Husband to Amy and son-in-law of Jack.

Maggie – Amazon Warrior from Tocabaga .
Mike – Friend of Jack Gunn and Tocabaga security agent.
Pete – Second in command of the new Templar order.
Quanah Iron Coat – Chief of the Comanche Nation.
Ragsdale – A bad guy in Indianola, who runs a whore house. He claimed to be Billy Bob's father.
Ron – Brother of Jack Gunn a Retired Navy vet. Part of Tocabaga security.
Rick – President of Tocabaga Association, security team member.
Sally – Girl friend of Walker, who owns a diner.
Tommy Gunn – Son of Jack Gunn and a retired Marine Scout Sniper.

OTHER BOOKS BY THOMAS H. WARD

THE TOCABAGA CHRONICLES:

TOCABAGA 1: Revised Edition

TOCABAGA 2: Theoterrorism

TOCABAGA 3: Warm Blood – Cold Steel

TOCABAGA 4: The Talos Warriors

TOCABAGA 5: The Quislings & Androktones

TOCABAGA 6: The Dimachaerus Clan - Missing In Action

TOCABAGA 7: Pàn Guó Zuì - High Treason

TOCABAGA 8: The Invisibles

TOCABAGA 9: The Crimson Cross

TOCABAGA 10: Power of the Sword

CONTACT THOMAS H. WARD:

Website: www.ThomasHWardBooks.com
Email: Tocabaga.Jack@gmail.com
Facebook: www.Facebook.com/Tocabaga

66023965R00093

Made in the USA
Charleston, SC
07 January 2017